REAL GOOD LOVE

Book Two of the REAL DUET

MEGHAN MARCH

Editor: Pam Berehulke, Bulletproof Editing
www.bulletproofediting.com

Cover design: @ by Hang Le
www.byhangle.com

Cover photo: @ Regina Wamba, Mae I Design
www.maeidesign.com

Interior Design: Stacey Blake, Champagne Formats
www.champagneformats.com

Visit my website at www.meghanmarch.com.

ABOUT THIS BOOK

I've had my fair share of bad boys, but nothing prepared me for what it was like to be with a real good man.

Logan Brantley changed everything.

Somewhere along the way, what started as a fling became the best part of my life. He makes me want all the things I've never had, like forever and happily ever after, but nothing worth having comes easily.

Everyone is betting on us to fail, but I'm ready to fight for this real good love.

Real Good Love is the conclusion of the Real Duet and should be read following *Real Good Man*.

ONE

Breaking news tonight from country star Holly Wix's hometown of Gold Haven, Kentucky. Although a small village of only about two thousand residents, it has been plagued by the methamphetamine epidemic that has impacted much of rural America. Sources in Gold Haven report the explosion of a third meth house in a matter of weeks, and we're told this one is located near a residence Wix owns and still visits on occasion.

Even more devastating to the town, an unidentified body has been discovered inside. No name has been released yet, pending notification of the family.

We'll have more as the story develops. We're sending our top investigative reporter, Memphis Lockwood, to Gold Haven to dig for answers. Stay tuned for her reports coming live from Kentucky.

Banner

BY THE TIME MY FLIGHT TOUCHES DOWN IN NEW York, I find myself feeling anxious. It's hard to believe I only left here a couple of weeks ago. The city that has been my home already feels foreign.

As I climb into the back of a cab at JFK, I rattle off the address of my old apartment building. I cringe as the driver slams on the brakes, honks his horn, and yells out the window at a Mercedes that cut him off. It's nothing like driving through the one blinking red light in Gold Haven. The people and cyclists cutting across the street force yet another abrupt stop, annoying me.

After the nauseating hour-long ride, I find myself wondering why I've always considered Manhattan the only truly livable city on the planet. Maybe because it's all I've ever really known, but Logan has shown me a completely different perspective. New York may be the center of the world in a lot of ways, but it's no longer the center of *my* world.

When I climb out of the cab in front of the building, the doorman's eyebrows shoot up.

"Ms. Regent. We've missed you. I hope you're doing well."

"Thank you, Joe. I'm doing great."

The lines around his eyes deepen as his quick smile dies away. "I assume you've heard about Mrs. Frances passing."

"That's why I'm here." Tears burn my eyes, but I blink them away.

"She always liked you. May not have acted like it, but she did. Do you need me to call up to the apartment, or are they expecting you?"

I shake my head. "Sofia asked me to come. I texted her on the way here."

He glances toward the elevator. "You know the way then."

With a small smile, I drag my suitcase toward the shiny

gold doors and press the call button. When it finally arrives, I step inside and select my old floor.

As the doors slide closed, a man shoves his briefcase between them to stop them. *Typical New York.* He and a woman bustle inside. He reaches for the button panel but yanks his hand back almost immediately without pressing one.

Are they the new tenants in my former apartment? My question is answered within moments when the man speaks.

"You must be helping clean out the apartment across the hall. We heard the old lady passed away."

My hackles rise at the way he refers to Myrna, even though I've called her *the old lady* plenty of times myself. But still, that was after years of the privilege of knowing her. These people don't know crap.

"Her name was Myrna Frances." My tone is frosty at best, dripping with an unspoken layer of *go fuck yourself.*

The woman presses a hand to her chest. "Are you family? We're terribly sorry for your loss. She seemed . . . lovely."

My hold on my temper snaps, weakened by grief and hours of travel. "I lived across the hall from her for five years, which is a hell of a lot more than you can say. Don't feed me your bullshit sympathy. You didn't know her."

Guilt settles in both their expressions as the woman's hand lowers to her rounded stomach. "We're sorry about that. I'm due in four months, and we really needed a bigger place. It wasn't personal. It was just . . . we needed the space more than you did."

Her words don't make sense . . . at first. But then the pieces snap together.

I open my mouth and close it again before finally speaking. "Are you . . . are you telling me that *you* sold me out to the association board and got me evicted so you could *have more space*?"

The woman recoils at my harsh tone. "Not us personally. A friend in the building who knew we couldn't stay in our place when the baby came. I've felt really guilty ever since, though."

A rusty laugh escapes my throat. "You've felt *guilty*? For making sure I ended up homeless?" I look down at her stomach and back up to her face as the elevator doors slide open. "God help your kid. I hope you're not as shitty of a parent as you are a person."

I stalk out of the elevator and down to Myrna's door, wrath fueling my every step. One of the tears I've been holding at bay sneaks through and lands on my cheek. I swipe it away, even more furious.

I've spent all this time being angry at Myrna, thinking she ratted me out, but it was some asshole trying to get a bigger place for a friend. The knowledge overwhelms me, and another tear falls.

My fist lands on the door harder than I intend, but I have to get out of this hallway before I let them see me cry. I don't turn to see if they're following or are wisely choosing to wait in the elevator until I'm out of sight.

Thankfully, Sofia opens the door and throws her arms around me. "I'm so glad you're here."

I hug her back hard as she begins to shake. Pulling away, I meet her tear-filled gaze, which matches my own. "Me too. I'm so sorry."

"It'll be better now. You're here, and I don't have to do

this alone." She sniffles as another tear tracks down her cheek. "Mrs. Frances's daughter just called and said she's not coming."

"What?" Rage and grief take turns slamming fist after fist into my gut. "What do you mean, she's not coming? Her mother died. She has to come."

Sofia shakes her head. "I don't understand either. She was so angry. She just yelled and yelled and hung up on me."

Myrna's relationship with her daughter is about as good as mine with my mother. And yet I still don't understand how she could decide she's opting out of this responsibility. If she's serious . . . that's *tragic*. But maybe that's how my mother would react if something happened to me. I can practically hear her.

"Now isn't a good time. I'm not able to leave until this segment of the research is concluded."

Not. Acceptable.

I wrap a hand around each of Sofia's shoulders and squeeze. "I'll call her. There's got to be some kind of mistake. Maybe she just delayed her flight because she had something going on."

I pull out my phone and find Dee Booker's contact information. She answers on the second ring.

"Hi, this is Banner Regent. You know, I used to live across—"

"Are you calling to tell me I should've visited more while she was alive, and maybe she wouldn't have screwed me over so hard in death?" She spits the angry words at me, not sounding at all like a congresswoman.

"I'm sorry, Ms. Booker. I know that this isn't easy. My

mother and I have a . . . difficult relationship too, but I would—"

"Am I supposed to care that you have mommy issues? If that's what you think this is, you are woefully mistaken."

Her jab about mommy issues hits home, and I stiffen. Myrna would be so embarrassed, and I'm embarrassed for her.

"Yeah, I do have mommy issues. Actually, I have shitty, disconnected parent issues. But that's not what *this* is about. Who do you think is going to handle Myrna's estate and apartment if you don't step up? She didn't ask a whole lot from you while she was alive; the least you could do is give her some consideration now that she's gone."

I almost expect lightning to strike me down because someone could say the same thing to me if my mom died tomorrow. Grief for a parent I haven't even lost yet rises up, and those few tears from earlier multiply.

Dee Booker is silent for a beat after I stop speaking. "You don't even know, do you?" A bitter laugh comes over the line. "I don't need to spare a moment of consideration for my mother because she didn't have any for me. After all, she left every damn thing to you."

TWO

Logan

THIS TIGHT DEADLINE ON THE MOST IMPORTANT project I've ever had is all that's keeping me from getting on a plane to New York to track Banner down and get answers from the source. I can't stop fucking thinking about the box of pregnancy tests I found in the bathroom.

As much as I want to call or text her to demand answers, this isn't the kind of conversation that's happening over the phone.

Before I can get lost in wrenching on the car, Jock yells over the beat of Boone Thrasher's latest album playing in the garage.

"Cop wants to talk to you, boss."

I jerk my head up and look in his direction. Sure enough, Cody Reeves is standing in the doorway between the waiting room and the shop.

Fuck. I toss the wrench into the top of my toolbox and yank the rag from the back pocket of my coveralls to wipe my hands. After turning down the stereo, I head in his direction.

"What can I do for you, Cody?" I ask as he backs up into the waiting room. Having a cop show up is never a good sign in my book. "You here about Jeff? Because I haven't seen him or talked to him."

"No. I got a few questions about a former employee of yours."

"Who?"

"Roy Planter. I understand you fired him a few months back."

My suspicions rise. *Roy?* What the fuck is going on with Roy? "Yeah, I fired him."

He pulls out his cop notepad. "Do you remember when that was?"

"I'd have to check my records. I don't recall the exact date."

"Can you tell me why you fired him?"

"He showed up drunk one too many times, and I couldn't have that kind of liability in my shop."

Cody makes a note and looks up. "When's the last time you saw him?"

"Why all the questions about Roy? What the hell is going on?"

"I need to know the last time you saw him, Logan."

"At Piggly Wiggly. He was checking out ahead of me a couple weeks ago. Haven't seen him since."

"His daughter says you never liked him."

I look up at the ceiling, trying for patience before I answer. "I fired the guy. It wasn't personal; it was business. Rachel's feelings on the matter don't count. She and everyone else in this town know Roy needs to have his ass in a seat at AA if he wants to get some help."

"That's not gonna happen. His body was identified this morning by his dental records."

Shock squeezes my chest like a vise. "What the fuck are you talking about?"

Cody closes his notepad and shoves it in his front pocket before he answers. "Roy Planter is dead. Seems he blew up himself and the old Nigel place early this morning."

I start putting the pieces together. "I heard about it on the radio on my way to work. He was cookin' meth?"

Cody gives me the cop shrug. "Allegedly. The crew is still going through the structure, but it was definitely a lab. Chief Timmons finally decided to take this shit seriously now that the national news is reporting on Gold Haven, so we've been told to investigate all possible avenues. We're getting famous again, but this time for all the wrong reasons."

I jam my hand into my hair. "Shit. What a fucking mess."

"Damn right it is. Thanks for answering my questions." Cody turns to walk toward the door, but pauses with his hand on the metal bar that stretches across the glass. "Is it just me, or does it seem like you've got connections to a lot of the people I'm investigating lately?"

I give him a hard look. "What are you trying to say, man? This is a small town. You could connect just about anyone to everyone else."

"I'm not trying to say anything, just making an observation. Have a good one, Logan."

He pushes open the door, leaving me standing in the waiting room with a punch of guilt. My hands clench into fists.

This isn't my fault.

Fuck.

———— ✻ ————

Six hours later, my stomach is gnawing on my spine, and I straighten from under the hood of Boone Thrasher's Olds 442. This restoration is testing my limits, including this stubborn carburetor. I back away from the car and wipe my hands. My back and shoulders are aching, and the only thing I want right now is a shower, a burger, a beer, and Banner. Not necessarily in that order.

I still haven't called her. I got a text from her to let me know she made it to New York, and I replied with a simple *Good to hear. Be safe.*

Maybe I'm naive for expecting her to bring up the subject of the pregnancy tests now that she's hundreds of miles away, considering she didn't bother to mention it when we were in the same bed last night. Either way, her lack of response is grating on me.

My phone rings as I finish scrubbing up with Fast Orange, and I dry my hands and reach for it.

Not Banner.

"What up, man?"

Granger Ryan, my best friend and Gold Haven's fire chief, says, "It's been a shit day. You wanna meet for a beer at Pints and Pins?"

"I heard about the fire and the body. Definitely a shit day. You get it handled all right?"

"Yeah, but I don't want to sit home and drink by myself. You up for it?"

"Sure. Give me forty-five minutes and I'll be there." Maybe this way I'll be able to keep myself from calling Banner to demand answers.

"Cool. See you then."

I hang up and look around my shop.

Someday, this place will be on the map, and I won't have to hustle so fucking hard to make sure it stays solidly in the black.

I cross the room to hit the lights and lock up.

Today just isn't that day.

THREE

Logan

"THIS SHIT IS ENOUGH TO MAKE ME HATE MY JOB. Do you know how much it fucking sucks to trip over a charred body?"

I drop the last bite of my burger in the red plastic basket on the table in front of me. The thought and visual of Roy Planter's remains has officially killed my appetite.

Granger lifts his beer and takes a swig. "Poor, stupid motherfucker. Shoulda known better. Got my ass out of bed at three a.m. to deal with his mess."

I reach for my beer. "Cody came around asking questions this morning. Wanting to know why I fired Roy."

Granger sets his beer on the table between us. "Because he was a drunk, and everyone knows you let him stay on way too long."

"That's what I told him."

"Makes you think about how fickle of a bitch this life is. One minute you're doing something stupid, and the next you're dead and your family finds out you're cooking meth."

"Any chance you're wrong about the meth?"

Granger shakes his head. "No. This is my third meth house in the last few weeks. The signs are impossible to miss. When we went to Lexington three years ago to train on this, I never thought I'd have to worry about all the extra steps we've gotta take, but now it's way too familiar."

"Do you think they're related?"

He shrugs. "I don't fucking know. It's not my job to figure out who set 'em, just to put 'em out. But damned if they're not pissing me off. No one thinks about me and my guys putting our asses on the line every time we ride out to a call. If this shit gets one of us killed, I'm gonna tear this town apart until I find out who's behind it. I don't need to be making a call to someone's wife or parents telling them some asshole cookin' meth is responsible for puttin' one of my guys in the ground."

"Hey, guys, can I get you anything?" Rosie, the cocktail waitress, asks as she stops at our table. Banner filled in for her on one of her first nights in Gold Haven.

Granger's gaze shoots across the room as a gust of wind blows through the doors, followed by a familiar laugh. I glance over to see Julianne coming in with one of her salon girls, Mary something. "Better get me another beer."

"I'll take one too."

Granger's attention shifts to Julianne as she comes toward us. Julianne braces as soon as she sees him, but doesn't slow her stride.

"Where are you hiding Banner today? She was supposed to come in for nails, and she canceled." Julianne pins her gaze on mine, completely ignoring Granger.

"She had to go back to New York to handle something."

"She's coming back here, though, right?"

13

The question crashes into me with the same force as the balls slamming into pins only a dozen feet away. My answer is fast and definite.

"Fuck yes, she's coming back." In my head, I add, *especially if she's pregnant with my kid.*

"I like her. It's nice to see at least one man can recognize a good thing when he has it." The taunt is pointed, and Julianne spins on her heel and continues to the bar.

Granger chugs the rest of his beer before shooting another look at Julianne's back. "Women are a fucking trap." He turns back to me. "What the hell are you doing getting tangled up with one from New York, anyway? Is that shit serious?"

I don't intend to say it, but the words come out. "It might be real fucking serious if I knocked her up."

Granger's eyes widen as he leans back in his chair and crosses his arms over his chest. "What the hell are you talking about?"

"I found a box of pregnancy tests in her bathroom this morning, and one was missing."

"And?"

"And nothing."

He leans forward, dropping his elbows on the table, and I'm grateful he keeps his voice low. "You didn't demand answers right then? What the hell, man? You know how women are. Looking to trap you any way they can."

This whole situation has been eating me all day, but I recognize the truth when I speak. "Banner isn't like that. She's not looking to trap me."

Granger's gaze narrows as he leans a few inches closer. "How do you know? She's got a job and money of her own?

Doesn't need your paycheck?"

"She has her own business."

"Successful?"

I reach for my beer. "Not yet. But she's working on it."

"So she doesn't have a job that actually brings in money, and you're still sure she's not trying to lock you down?" He leans back in his chair again, an expectant look on his face.

Even with the facts objectively stacking up against her, there's no way I can pin that motive on Banner. The more I think about it, the more I realize she's exactly the opposite of the women I've dodged in Gold Haven. My New York City princess would run far and fast in the opposite direction if she thought she was trapped in Kentucky because she got knocked up by a mechanic. Or in this case, stay in New York . . .

Fuck.

"She's not like that. You'll see when you meet her." Even though my words sound confident, I wonder what the hell I'm going to have to do to make sure Banner does come back. *I'll drive my ass up there and haul her home if I have to.*

"Whatever you say, man. I'm done with women except for a quick fuck these days."

Rosie comes back with our beers, and we change the subject to college basketball.

As I'm walking out of Pints and Pins, my phone buzzes in my pocket, finally, with a text from the woman who seems to be constantly on my mind.

BANNER NYC: It's been a long crazy day. I have a ton of

stuff to tell you, but I'm drained tonight. Talk tomorrow?

I climb in my truck and tap out my response.

LOGAN: *Yeah. We need to start talking about all of it.*
BANNER NYC: *We will. Night. xo*
LOGAN: *Night, Bruce.*

I fire up my truck and turn in the direction of my empty house, frustrated that I'm not getting any resolution on this subject tonight.

FOUR

Banner

I WALK INTO MYRNA'S LAWYER'S OFFICE THE NEXT morning, not knowing what to expect.

"Banner Regent to see Gregory Lowenstein," I tell the receptionist when I walk up to the desk.

"Of course, Ms. Regent. He's expecting you. Let me tell him you're here."

As the young blonde picks up the phone to call to announce my presence, I take a few steps toward the window, staring out at the New York skyline. It's gray and cloudy, which fits my mood perfectly.

"Ms. Regent?"

I turn, and the receptionist indicates that I should follow her. I trail behind her to a nondescript conference room with a large wooden table matching the paneled walls. It's also empty.

"Mr. Lowenstein will be right in," she says. "Just one moment. Can I bring you something to drink?"

"Espresso would be great."

"Of course."

Moments after she shuts the door behind her, it swings open again.

"Well, Ms. Regent, somehow you charmed my client. I'd love to know how you did it." A man of average height wearing glasses, with a shiny spot in the middle of his gray ring of hair, smiles and holds out his hand. "I'm Greg Lowenstein, and I've been Ms. Frances's lawyer for twenty-some years."

Twenty years of being at Myrna's beck and call? I'm not sure I could handle it.

"It's a pleasure to meet you. I wouldn't exactly say I charmed her. More like I drove her absolutely insane."

Lowenstein holds up a hand. "For her, it was kind of the same thing. She was a great old lady, sharp as a tack, but her tongue was too, as I'm sure you well know. I heard everything about everyone because she called once a week to change her will. That vibrator incident almost cost you a chunk of change."

Oh my God. She told her lawyer about that? Peeking at the conference room table, I wonder if there's room to crawl under it.

"As much of my time as Myrna took up, I'm sincerely going to miss her. Well, my billable hours are going to miss her, and my secretary is going to have to find a new source of entertainment. So, how about we get started?" He opens a file and starts running through the estate plan and how things work.

I zone out almost immediately at all the legal jargon. Why don't lawyers just use regular words? Do they get paid more for using the big ones?

I raise a hand like a second grader to stop him. *Please,*

God, stop.

Thankful when he takes a breath to pause, I jump in. "I get it. Myrna's estate plan was super fancy because you charged her a crap ton of money to work on it and keep changing it. But bottom-line it for me, Greg. What do I really need to know?"

He takes off his glasses and lays them on the table. "Thirty."

"Thirty what?" I ask, wondering if there's some legal definition for it that I'm not aware of.

"Thirty million. That's what you've inherited in various investment accounts, not including the apartment or other property. For those, we can only go from market-value estimates—"

I raise my hand again, this time like a really rich second grader.

"Are you shitting me?" I say as I lower my hand.

"No, Ms. Regent, I'm not, in your vernacular, shitting you."

"Holy fucking shit."

"Indeed."

I discreetly slide one hand under my arm and pinch myself. *Crap, that hurts.* Not dreaming. Okay, then . . .

I whip my head around to check for cameramen jumping out to surprise me.

None.

"You're not joking."

Mr. Lowenstein shakes his head. "No. I don't joke about lunch or money."

I hope he meant love and money, but I don't ask. I'm still trying to wrap my head around the fact that Myrna's daughter wasn't completely full of it when she told me Myrna left me everything.

"Why would she do this? It makes no sense at all."

"She liked you."

I meet his gaze. "She liked her dog. She tolerated me."

"Speaking of the dog, you're the trustee of the Jordana Frances Pet Trust, although you did not inherit her."

"Please tell me it was Sofia."

"Indeed."

So I didn't inherit *everything*, but *holy shit*.

I pay a lot closer attention to what Lowenstein says for the rest of the meeting, which means my brain feels like it's going to explode by the end of it.

Part of me expected Dee Booker was exaggerating, so even though I was ready for some kind of inheritance from Myrna, I wasn't expecting *this*.

I walk out of the office and barely notice the crowds of people around me as I wander in the direction of my hotel, still reeling with shock.

Out of habit, I pull out my phone to call Greer and tell her the news, but she doesn't answer. Her new life is taking off in LA, and while I couldn't be happier that my friend has found happiness, I selfishly miss having her around.

I miss Myrna too. Last night, I couldn't handle staying in her apartment surrounded by her things, so I hauled my suitcase to the Parker Meridian and sank into the bathtub . . . and cried.

Grief battered me as I recalled our exchanges, and how much it bothered me that I didn't clear the air with her on the phone. She had no clue I left New York upset with her. Maybe it's a plus that she didn't die thinking we had unfinished business. Although, if she'd known, maybe she would have hung on a hell of a lot longer.

Why did I jump to conclusions? I should have just asked her. Myrna was nothing if not brutally honest with me.

I toasted her with almost the entire contents of the minibar, which she's ironically now paying for, and passed out on a tearstained pillow.

When I woke up this morning, my head hammering, I rolled over looking for Logan, but the hotel decor reminded me I was a long way from Gold Haven. I left Kentucky a broke-ass CEO, and now I'm a legit baller.

Well, I will be after who knows how many more meetings with lawyers and financial people who will finalize all the details and wind down Myrna's affairs.

Not to mention, I have to figure out what to do with all of her stuff. She was a pack rat of the first order, and to say I'm overwhelmed by the thought of digging through all of it is the understatement of the century.

I wrap my coat around me tighter as I pause on the corner of Fifth Avenue. For the first time in longer than I can remember, I have zero urge to go inside any of my favorite stores and shop.

Which is ironic, considering I could snap my fingers and demand one of everything now. My new bank account wouldn't even blink.

Two women burst through the doors of a store, laughing and carrying armloads of bags. I step out of their way, but can't help but overhear their conversation as they turn toward Starbucks.

"That top you got will be perfect for the club opening tonight. Your tits will look amazing. I can't wait to post pictures so everyone who can't get in will be jealous."

They both giggle—annoyingly, I might add—before the other responds. "God, I'm due for a good fuck too. I'm taking home the hottest guy I see."

"Damn, girl. Get it. But buh-bye in the morning, right?"

"Obvi. You know how I am."

The two women disappear into Starbucks, and someone knocks into me from behind. The signal has changed, which means I need to move my ass across the street. Shaking myself out of my momentary eavesdropping session, I stride forward, but their words stay with me.

Not so very long ago, that was me.

How cringe-worthy and superficial.

Who would have thought a guy from Kentucky I was never supposed to meet would change *my life.*

I haven't been gone long, but I legitimately miss Logan. I step into a doorway and pull out my phone to text him. He's busy working on Boone Thrasher's car, but I can't help it. Other than Greer, he's the only person I want to tell about all of this stuff. In fact, I wanted to tell him last night, but I kept my message vague in case Myrna's daughter was full of shit.

But she wasn't.

BANNER: *You know how I said I had big news? I really need to tell you about it.*

Not expecting an immediate reply, I slide my phone into my purse, but pause when it vibrates.

Except it's not Logan. It's my ob-gyn, who also happens to be my college roommate's older sister.

DR. LADY LIPS: *Do you have any questions about anything?*

I don't claim to be mature when it comes to my contact-naming skills, but at least I'm not confusing her with anyone else. Also, *shit.*

BANNER: *Crap! I left before it came, but I'm in NYC right now.*

DR. LADY LIPS: *I can squeeze you in at noon tomorrow, but you better bring me sushi.*

BANNER: *I'll be there. BTW, I still laugh every time you text me.*

DR. LADY LIPS: *YOU TOLD ME YOU CHANGED MY CONTACT INFORMATION.*

BANNER: *I lied.*

DR. LADY LIPS: *No sushi for you.*

FIVE

Logan

BANNER NYC: You know how I said I had big news? I really need to tell you about it.

I've been staring at the text for five minutes, wondering why in the hell she thinks this is the right way to tell me she's fucking pregnant. But this is Banner, and she doesn't do anything the normal way.

I finally tap out a reply.

LOGAN: Shouldn't we talk about it in person?

I wait, phone in hand next to the 442, for a response.

BANNER NYC: I can't wait that long. I have to figure out what I'm doing, and I want your input.

What in the actual fuck?

She has to *figure out what she's doing*? Somehow over

the last twenty-four hours, I've gone from shock and disbelief to acceptance and even . . . excitement over the possibility of Banner being pregnant.

The idea that she might decide not to have the kid guts me.

It's never been my goal to be a dad, especially right now when my business is still in the early stages, but shockingly I'm okay with the idea when the woman in question is Banner. I knew I was in deep before, but this seals it for me. And she's fucking right that she's not making any decisions before we talk.

LOGAN: Call me.

BANNER NYC: Give me twenty minutes. I'll call when I'm back at my hotel.

Her hotel? I thought she was staying at the old lady's place?

Granger's words from last night run through my head. *So she doesn't have a job that actually brings in money, and you're still sure she's not trying to lock you down?*

Why would Banner drop money she doesn't have on a hotel when she could stay somewhere for free? Even though it hasn't been long, I'm getting to know how Banner works. Wherever she picked to stay can't be cheap. I'm not sure any place is in New York.

Right now, nothing makes any fucking sense.

The next twenty minutes are the longest ones in my goddamned life.

SIX

Banner

I LET MYSELF INTO MY HOTEL ROOM AND DROP MY STUFF on the desk before flopping backward onto the fluffy white duvet with my phone in hand.

When I checked in last night, I was a tiny bit worried about how I was going to pay the bill if Dee Booker was full of crap, but that's one worry I no longer have. I tap on Logan's contact to call him, and he answers before the first ring is complete.

"You're never going to believe what I'm about to tell you," I say in lieu of a greeting.

"You'd be surprised what I'd believe," Logan says, his drawl sounding more pronounced, or maybe it's just the fact that I've been hearing only clipped New Yorkers today.

"You know how I thought Frau Frances got me evicted from my apartment because she wanted to get rid of me?"

"Yeah . . ." Confusion colors his tone.

"I was wrong. It was actually this couple who straight-up admitted that they needed more room because they're having a baby. Total assholes. But that doesn't matter anymore, because it turns out that Myrna didn't want to get rid of me. She actually left me everything. Thirty million dollars and the apartment and a bunch of other stuff that I haven't totally grasped yet."

"What?" Logan sounds like he's choking.

"I know, right?"

"She left you everything?"

I nod, even though he can't see me. "Everything."

"What about her daughter?"

Every time I think about how shocked Dee Booker must have been when she learned her mother left everything to a former neighbor, my heart does this painful clenching thing, because I can almost picture it happening to me. The call from my mom's lawyer saying that her last thought of me was . . . nothing.

"She didn't leave her anything."

"How is that even possible? I thought you said she hated you?"

I sit up on the bed and rise to my feet to start pacing the room. "I was wrong, I guess. The lawyer made it sound like she changed her mind all the time."

Mentally, I'm kicking myself again for not clearing the air before she died. I hate that we left so many things unsaid. And she didn't get a chance to see the final sex-toy lineup of Blush.

"Thirty million . . ." A layer of awe has slipped into Logan's voice. "Holy fucking shit."

"That's basically what I said. I have to meet with her lawyer again, and her financial people, to sort all this stuff out and transfer it all over, so I'm going to be here longer than I planned. I had no idea Frau Frances had so much shit, which means now *I* have that much shit, and I have to figure out what I'm going to do with it." I pause to take a breath. "But before you ask, I'm not staying in New York. I'm coming back."

"Goddamned right you're coming back. I don't care how much money you've got, I will drive up there and—"

Logan's adamant tone catches me off guard, and I interrupt.

"Calm down, Wolverine. No need to get the claws out. You won't have to come drag me back. I realized a few things."

I take another breath, preparing myself to get real with him. This isn't a typical Banner activity, so I'm probably going to screw it up.

"Even though Myrna just handed me the opportunity to stay in New York and go back to the life I had, I don't want that life. Before, I thought New York had everything, but now I know it doesn't have the one thing I really want. You."

My heart hammers at my declaration. This is as close as I've gotten to admitting that I'm kinda crazy in love with Logan, and even though I've promised myself I wasn't going to say it first, I need him to know this.

When all I get is silence, panic creeps in. "You can say something now. Really, anytime."

"I'm waiting for you to tell me the rest," Logan says, his tone less harsh than before, but there's something in it I can't identify.

"The rest of what?"

Logan takes a breath before he speaks. "That you're pregnant."

I spin around and slam my shin into the bed frame. "Shit!" I yell, jumping back on one foot and losing my grip on my phone. It lands perfectly on the corner before sliding across the floor. I dive after it, snagging it just before it hits the dresser.

But I'm too late. The screen is shattered.

"Fuck!"

I sit up, wrap one hand on my screaming shinbone, and stare down at my poor phone. Behind the shattered glass, the screen is black. The call is dropped. I hit the power button and wait for it to come back on, but nothing happens.

"You've got to be shitting me," I say to the empty room. "There is no way my luck is this bad."

But two minutes of pressing buttons with absolutely no sign of life from my phone tells me otherwise.

I reach for the hotel phone and then replace it in the cradle. I don't know Logan's number. I don't know anyone's freaking number anymore.

Shit. Shit. Shit.

Laptop. Google. *I'll find the number for his shop.*

I tap my nails on the desk as I wait for my laptop to boot up, and by the time I connect to the hotel Wi-Fi and pull up my browser, I'm ready to tear my hair out. Patience has never been one of my virtues, and that's not changing today.

Thankfully, Google provides the number to his shop, and I call it.

No answer, and the voice mail is full, so I can't even leave a message.

"Logan, you need to check your goddamned voice mails!"

I call again. And again. And again.

Finally, someone picks up. "Hello?"

I can barely hear him over the sound of country music. "Why in the hell do you think I'm pregnant?"

"Who is this?" the man asks, and I realize it's not Logan.

"I need to talk to your boss. Now."

"Logan?"

"Yes!"

"Hold on. He's busy."

"He's definitely not too busy for this call, so you just march over there and hand him the phone."

"Calm down, lady. I'm working on it."

I barely restrain myself from ripping into the guy for being rude, but I've got more important matters to deal with. The music in the background goes silent finally, and I can hear the man say, "There's someone on the phone for you, boss, and she sounds pissed. You knock someone up?"

Logan's voice finally comes on the line. "Banner?"

"If there's a question of whether you knocked up more than just me, we're going to have a serious problem, Logan Brantley."

"Why the hell did you hang up on me? And just freaking tell me—are you are pregnant?"

"I dropped my phone and it broke. I didn't hang up. And no! Of course not. I told you I'm on birth control. I've been eating home cooking for two freaking weeks, but I'm not fat, so what the hell?"

Logan releases a long breath. "Then why did you have a box of pregnancy tests on the counter in your bathroom with one missing?"

Everything finally falls together, and I pinch the bridge

of my nose. "Because my ob-gyn was probably breaking some laws when she said she'd mail me the birth control shot to give myself, but I had to take a pregnancy test first to confirm I was good to go."

"You're fucking kidding me." From the tone of Logan's voice, I can tell this isn't the response he expected.

"Why didn't you just ask?"

"Because this isn't the kind of shit you talk about over the phone. This is the kind of shit you talk about in person."

He has a good point. "So you were going to wait and wonder until I got back?"

"Yeah, but when you said you had to decide what you were going to do, I couldn't wait."

Realization dawns. "You thought I'd have an abortion? Without ever talking to you about anything? Jesus, Logan, thanks for the vote of confidence."

"Look, it's your body and your choice, but you better believe I would've had something to say about it if you were going to go through with something like that."

"I'm not pregnant, so we can stop right here. But for the record, there's no way in hell I would do that. I couldn't."

"Well, that's good to know."

The ridiculousness of the whole situation hits me hard, and laughter rises up in my chest. "I can't believe you thought I was pregnant."

"You better not be laughing about this right now. If I could reach you, I'd spank that ass of yours for making me wonder."

"You have to admit that it is kind of funny." I pause as tears stream down my face. "Or maybe I'm just an emotional freaking wreck because of everything else." My laughter dies, but the tears continue.

"Fuck, baby. I hate hearing you cry. Especially when I'm not close enough to hold you. Shhh, it's gonna be all right. I promise."

I walk to the bathroom to grab a tissue and sniff back another wave of tears. "I'm sorry. It's been a little bit of an emotional roller coaster lately."

"A little bit? Bruce, I think you're making a hell of an understatement there."

"It's just . . . God, you should have heard her daughter. She was so pissed. It's like she hated her."

"Not everyone gets along with their parents," Logan offers.

"I'm walking proof." I pause. "But I'd like to think there's no way I'd be so cold if someone called me tomorrow and told me my parents were dead."

"She's probably dealing with it her own way. Everyone does."

"I know. But I feel sorry for her, and I don't ever want someone to feel sorry for me like that."

"This may not be a suggestion you want to hear, but have you thought about going to see your parents while you're there to try to mend fences?"

I think about it before replying. "I don't know if I'm ready yet. They didn't think twice about leaving me to face being evicted by myself."

"That's shitty, but if there's anything I've learned lately, it's that we've got no guarantees in this life. You might have to step up and be the bigger person."

"Maybe you're right."

"Even a blind squirrel finds a nut now and again."

"I miss you," I blurt out.

Logan chuckles softly into the phone. "I miss you too, Bruce. Do you have any idea how long it's going to take to get everything in order up there?"

"Not really. I need to clean out the apartment and figure out what to do with Myrna's stuff, and that's alongside straightening out all the financial and legal things, which is way easier to do here in person, I think."

"I believe you. Take the time you need to get it sorted out. You know I've got plenty of work to keep me buried until this project is done, and I'll be waiting here when you get back."

Relief that Logan understands the position I'm in sweeps through me. "How did you get to be so amazing?"

Logan laughs, and I love the sound of it. "I'm not amazing. You are, Bruce."

"Can I call you later? I've gotta go buy a new phone and come up with a plan of attack for the apartment so I can work through this as quickly as possible."

"You can call me anytime. I'll even give you my number again."

"Logan Brantley's giving me his number," I purr. "I feel so special."

"That's because you are. Now, you feel free to remind all those New York guys that you've got a man at home, and he doesn't share."

I laugh, but there's something about his words that fills my chest with warmth. Gold Haven and Logan are home for me now. "He doesn't, huh?"

"My pie. I don't share my pie."

"You sound like—"

"A man staking his claim?" Logan interrupts. "That's because I am. You better not have a single doubt about that."

"Then you better make sure all those women in Gold Haven know that Logan Brantley's got all the pie he needs because he is taken." I emphasize the last three words, and it feels good to stake my own claim.

"Fair is fair, but that goes without saying. Call me later, Bruce." He rattles off his number, and I jot it down before giving him the one to my room.

I look up in the mirror after I hang up, and I'm not sure I've ever seen this big of a smile on my own face before.

I'm in deep.

SEVEN

Banner

"**M**YRNA WAS A DIRTY BIRDY!"

After the highs of this morning, sorting through Myrna's apartment all afternoon has been a definite low. At least until I open her nightstand drawer and find her collection of old-lady smut. Hidden underneath her bible is a stack of bodice rippers circa 1980 with titles like *Taken by the Sheik, His Captive Princess,* and *The Pirate's Prize.*

I hold them up for Sofia, who covers her mouth and laughs.

"No. Way."

I'm sure Myrna would be rolling in her grave right now if her daughter hadn't decided to have her cremated almost immediately and without a funeral. Grief and tears rise up at not having a chance to say a proper good-bye, but I shove them down. I'll find a way to make a fitting tribute to her some way, and in the meantime, it's easier for me to focus on the positives. Like the fact that Myrna had a strong love of capture romances.

Immediately my brain clicks into marketing mode . . .

What if I were to market to romance readers who need a little help with their one-handed reads? I grab my phone and make a few notes about the idea. Oh, and what if I rename the products for different types of lovers—the Sheik, the Billionaire, the Bad Boy, the Real Good Man.

The handheld heroes of Blush you can keep in your own bedroom.

There's no doubt which I prefer.

I set the books aside, deciding to keep them for my own collection—for research purposes, obviously—and continue through the drawers.

I found the big black cock earlier in the closet on the top shelf. With the silver accents, it could definitely be renamed the Billionaire. Apparently it was too much for Myrna, which is fine by me, because I'm not sure I could handle the visual anyway.

I arrange for all of her clothes, well-made but twenty years old, to be picked up tomorrow by a company specializing in redistributing them to people in need. I keep her favorite Burberry scarf and hat, though, as well as a sweater for Jordana to curl up on.

Myrna would be horrified, but I'm pretty sure she'd get over it if she knew how heartbroken her dog is right now. Luckily, the pup has her own trust, and Sofia is excited to take care of her.

A few more hours of sorting is all I can take before I've had enough. I've got a stack of boxes I'm shipping to Myrna's daughter, whether she likes it or not, because it doesn't seem right to throw the family memories away.

Sofia is feeding Jordy in the kitchen when I go in search

of her.

"I'm done for today. I'll be back tomorrow."

She lowers the pink dog-food bowl to the floor. "Me too. I'm exhausted even thinking about how much more there is to go through."

That's the understatement of the day. Two of Myrna's three bedrooms are packed with stuff, not to mention closets and cupboards. She had a lot of years to accumulate things, though, so I guess it makes sense.

"You sure you're good with staying here again tonight?" I ask Sofia as I wind down for the day.

She dusts her hands off on a rag. "I'm not quite ready to say good-bye yet."

"I know what you mean." I give her a quick hug before donning my coat and heading out the door. It's strange to be back in this building, especially knowing part of it is mine and no one can take it from me this time.

Deciding to walk instead of take a cab, I tuck my hands into my pockets and disappear into the crowd of people going home from work. I don't miss being one of them.

I pick up sushi from a favorite place and carry it with me, even though I'm supposed to bring some to Dr. Lady Lips, aka Dr. Brennan, for lunch tomorrow. Not having sushi is one of the things I really miss in Kentucky, so having it twice in two days is no hardship. But then again, watching a sushi chef doesn't compare to the visual of Logan grilling a steak to perfection.

Dammit, I miss him.

This is still all so new to me, and I'm lost in my thoughts until I'm nearly to the hotel.

"Banner! Banner!"

I look around to find who's calling my name. It's unusual enough that there's little to no chance of whoever it is calling to someone else.

A tap on my shoulder has me spinning around to face Brandon Sidewalk, a guy I went out with once to a club opening, who didn't understand that a short skirt was not an invitation to feel me up.

Unfortunately, he's standing there with a stupid grin on his face, so I can't exactly walk away. But I can pretend I don't remember him.

"I'm sorry. Do I know you?"

His brow furrows. "Brandon Smith. We went out a few weeks back to the opening of Olivesque. I've been meaning to text you to see if you wanted to go out again."

I pretend to dig through my memory bank before letting a look of recognition pass over my face. "Oh, you mean the guy who tried to shove his hand up my skirt without an invitation?"

He takes a step back, shock lighting his eyes. "Uh. Ah. Well . . ."

I narrow my gaze on him. "Yeah, that's what I thought. If you ever want to know how a real man acts with a woman, I'll let you talk to my boyfriend. Actually, on second thought, he'd probably toss your body down a mine shaft for trying that, so maybe in the interest of making sure he doesn't spend the next ten to fifteen in state prison, we'll keep this between us."

He stiffens, and genuine fear radiates from him as he clears his throat. "Sorry. I guess you're right. I don't know you."

As Brandon Sidewalk turns and walks away, I wonder

what I ever saw in the guy to make me accept even a single date. His shoulders barely fill out his suit jacket. His shoes and watch might cost more than some used cars, but they're pretentious as hell. I know he only bought them because they're designer.

My list of Brandon's shortcomings slams to a halt when I realize what I called Logan. *My boyfriend.*

It's been a long time since I've referred to anyone by that label. I continue toward the glass doors of the hotel as I turn it over in my head. *Does he consider me his girlfriend? We've never even talked about it. And why would we?*

Part of me wants to ask him, and the other part thinks the question is ridiculous. Then again, he thought he knocked me up, so I guess we've crossed over some imaginary relationship line, right? I still have no final conclusion when I let myself into my room, set my sushi on the desk, and remove my coat.

Halfway through what they should call an orgasm roll, my new phone rings. I grab it, thinking it's Logan, but it's Greer.

"Hey, stranger!"

"Hey, trouble. Sorry I missed your call this morning. It's been crazy out here. Also, LA traffic can go screw itself."

"I still can't believe you want to live there."

"It wasn't exactly a tough choice when I considered what was important."

A few weeks ago, I wouldn't have understood what she meant, but now I do. It's strange how much can change in such a short time.

"I get what you mean."

"So, are you going to spill? What's going on? Are you

loving Gold Haven?"

"I'm actually back in New York."

The phone goes silent for a moment. "Already? You can't tell me you're bored with Logan."

I steel myself to say the words that don't seem to be getting any easier. "No. Myrna Frances, my old across-the-hall neighbor, passed away."

"The old bat? The one who got you evicted?" Greer asks, confusion clear in her tone.

"Yeah, except she didn't get me evicted. She . . . actually, she left me everything, including her apartment."

Another silence falls between us.

"Are you shitting me?" It seems to be the most astute question to ask when it comes to what happened.

"Not shitting you. I don't have more money than you, but I've got a lot now."

"I'm so sorry to hear she passed, but wow. That's just . . . crazy. So you're staying in Manhattan for good now?"

My answer is quick and unequivocal. "No. At least, I don't plan to right now."

"So that means things are going well with Logan?"

"Things are good. I *like* him, Greer. This is all-new territory for me."

I don't have to tell her that last bit because there's no doubt that she already knows how unusual this is.

"How big is his dick?"

I choke on the spit in my mouth when my friend shoots me a question that would be more characteristic coming from me. "Did you really just ask that?"

"You would."

"True. Friends shouldn't let friends settle for guys with

small penises."

For some reason, with Logan as the subject, I find my-self less willing to share than I have been in the past.

"Oh my God, you don't want to tell me," Greer says. "Either it's really freaking small or you really do *like him, like him*. And if I know you, there's no way you'd fall for a guy with a small penis. It's against the Banner Regent handbook."

"I don't have a handbook."

"But if you did . . ."

She has a point. "All I'm going to say is this. He's got Congo *beat*."

Greer sucks in a breath because she's also fluent in the country-by-country penile-size comparison research. Mostly because we made it a game to memorize it just in case we both got to travel extensively and wanted to be sure we had the best chance of getting the good dick.

"Holy shit. I have to go look outside to see if people are ice skating, because I think hell just froze over. You really do like him."

"I'm so fucked, Greer."

"Why? It's not a bad thing."

"He lives in Kentucky."

"And so do you," she points out.

"For now. But what if . . ." I trail off.

"What if what? What are you worried about?"

It's time to face my fear. "What if he realizes I'm not enough for him?"

Another beat of silence passes before she responds. "I may have only met Logan Brantley once, but he didn't strike me as a stupid man. You're more than enough. He's fucking lucky that you're with him. You are a prize, Banner. Don't ever forget it."

In that moment, I'm reminded that sometimes you just need a pep talk from your best friend to set your world straight.

"You're right. I am."

"Good girl. Now, get your attitude back in place before we completely swap roles here."

"I love you, G."

"I love you, B."

"I miss you. Don't be a stranger."

"Same to you. Now, go call that man and have some filthy phone sex so he's thinking about you all night while you're hundreds of miles away."

"Damn, look at you being the dirty girl. It suits you."

"Yeah, I guess it does."

We say our good-byes and hang up.

I contemplate her suggestion while I finish my sushi, and then open my texts with Logan.

BANNER: *Can you talk?*

My phone vibrates in my hand thirty seconds later with a call rather than a text.

"Hey, Bruce."

"Hi."

"You've got some good timing. I'm just taking a quick break before I dive back into work."

I look at the clock. It's almost seven in Gold Haven. "How's the project going?"

"I've got a shit load more work to do on this car than

I thought. We're all hustling, and I'm putting in more time than anyone because that's how it goes. How are things up there?"

"I put in a lot of time at Myrna's. It's . . . harder than I expected." The burn of tears stings behind my eyes.

Logan's voice softens. "Of course it is, babe. She might've been a crotchety old lady, but she was your crotchety old lady."

He's exactly right. "I think what makes it harder is that I let her die thinking something horrible about her. That's not something I'll ever be able to change. It's been driving me crazy." A sniffle escapes, and I'm sure the tears will follow.

"Baby, I'm sorry. I wish I could hold you and tell you all the right things."

I snuffle again. "It's okay. I know it's my fault. I just have to live with it."

"She'd be proud of you, Banner. She wouldn't have left you everything if she was holding a grudge."

I think back to what the lawyer told me about Myrna changing her will almost weekly. "Or maybe she just didn't have time to change her mind."

"Stop, Bruce. Don't beat yourself up over it. Learn from it. Honor her memory by carrying out her wishes."

"How'd you get so smart about stuff like this?"

"I lost a lot of brothers, and death never gets easier. All you can do is try to do better in the future if you leave something unfinished in the past."

The tears are drying up, and I go on to tell him about the romance novels and Jordana staying here with Sofia.

"I like dogs. I've always worked too much to have one,

and I didn't want to be the kind of business where I had one sleeping in the waiting room all the time. If Sofia doesn't want to take her, you can bring her home."

Home. He says it so easily because that's what it is for him.

Is it mine now too? Because New York feels less and less like my home every hour that I'm here.

"I'll ask her and let you know."

"That sounds like a plan." He yawns into the phone.

"You're working too hard."

"No such thing when you own your own business."

"Did you even stop to eat?" As soon as my question is out, another thought follows. Emmy Harris better not try anything while I'm gone. We covered the *pie* situation, but I wouldn't put anything past her.

Logan Brantley is nobody's fool and picks up on my tone. "What are you really asking?"

I'm not beating around the bush. "Did Betty Crocker Barbie try to bring you a picnic basket tonight because I'm not around?"

He laughs, and I want to punch him for it. "Jealous, Bruce?"

I force out a laugh of my own. "Of course not. I mean, no more jealous than you'd be if I told you I saw Brandon Sidewalk outside the hotel."

Logan's laugh dies. "That fucker who tried to put his hand up your skirt?"

It actually shocks me that he remembers that, and so quickly. "You remember that?"

"Of course I remember the list of guys I'll need to take care of if I ever meet them."

Something about his macho words gets me going. "Oh yeah? So you are jealous?"

"I told you, that's my pie. I don't share my pie with anyone."

"And I told you I don't share either."

"You throw attitude at me like that when you're around, it's gonna be hard for me not to want to fuck it right out of you."

Instantly my panties are soaked, and I remember Greer's advice about filthy phone sex.

"Are you in the garage all by yourself?"

"Of course."

"Is your cock hard?"

Logan releases a breath and turns the question around on me. "Is your pussy wet?"

"Dripping."

He groans into the phone. "Fuck, baby. I wish I had you riding my face right now so I could taste all that sweetness. And for the record, I'm rock fucking hard."

I picture Logan in the garage, his hand in his ripped jeans as he jacks his cock. "I wish I could see you."

"Strip. I want you naked, lying on the bed, legs spread so you can bury your fingers deep in that sweet pussy. I want to hear you make yourself come as I tell you how fucking sexy you are."

I put the phone on speaker and drop it on the bed so I can peel off my jeans, shirt, panties, and bra. After tearing the duvet off the bed, I move the phone up higher and prop myself up on a pillow.

"If you could see me right now, you'd know that I'm doing exactly that." My fingers trail down my body to slide through my wetness.

Normally, if I were doing this without a phone audience, I'd tease myself more, but with Logan's words echoing in my head, there's no need.

His low growl comes through the phone at the same time as my index finger circles my clit. I plunge two fingers inside.

"How tight are you?"

"So tight, but I want more."

"You want my cock, don't you?"

"Yes."

"Did you bring one of your toys with you?"

"I never leave home without one."

"Go get it."

I pop off the bed, eager to follow his orders because I need this orgasm more than I need vodka. And that's saying a lot.

Once I've retrieved a prototype from my bag, I return to the bed and the phone. "I'm ready."

"Lay back down, spread your legs, and tease yourself."

"Are you jacking yourself off right now, Logan? I need a visual."

"I'm strangling my cock with my fist, but it's nothing compared to how hard your pussy grips me when you come."

I moan, loving his dirty words.

"That's right, baby. Tease that pussy, because you're going to fuck it and we're gonna come at the same time. I want the whole fucking city of New York to hear you scream my name."

I writhe on the bed, the vibrations of the toy on my clit

already dragging me toward the edge, but I need it inside me.

"I'm ready."

"You're ready when I say you are."

"Please, Logan."

"Fuck, I love the sound of you begging. Push it inside; tell me how it feels."

I slide the vibrator into my slick entrance, and kick up the intensity of the G-spot massager.

"Oh God. This won't take long," I tell him, my voice shaking.

"Fucking right it won't. You feel it on your G-spot?"

"Yes. Oh my God, yes."

"Don't forget to play with that sweet little clit. This is gonna go fast and hard."

I reach down and toy with my clit as I fuck myself with the vibrator. My moans are met with Logan's heavy breathing as he jacks himself off.

"I wish I could see you, but I can picture you in my mind, and you're so fucking beautiful."

The tidal wave of pleasure surges. "I'm not going to last long."

"You don't need to. Come hard, baby. Come hard and let me hear it."

I kick up the vibrations to the next level, and my scream pierces the room. "Logan!"

He groans loudly into the phone, followed by garbled words, and I picture thick, ropy jets of semen landing on the hood of a car. *Who knew that would be so sexy?*

I pull the vibrator away as aftershocks rip through me, and curl up on my side. "Did you come on a car?"

"I'll never tell."

"Did I scream loud enough?"

I can hear the smile in his voice when he replies. "It'll do for now, but this isn't going to be the last time."

"What did you say when you came? I couldn't understand."

A few beats pass before he replies. "Something I'd rather tell you in person."

EIGHT

Banner

A week later

BANNER: *I think I want to buy a pony now that I'm a legit millionaire.*

MY SEXY MAN: *Ponies don't cost millions. They're a dime a dozen down here.*

BANNER: *A unicorn?*

MY SEXY MAN: *Bruce . . .*

BANNER: *And I don't mean a pony that has something pointy just stuck to its head. No cheating.*

MY SEXY MAN: *Bruce . . .*

BANNER: *What? How is this unreasonable?*

MY SEXY MAN: *We'll find you a really expensive pony.*

BANNER: *A pink one?*

MY SEXY MAN: *I'll pick up some Rit dye at Walmart.*

BANNER: *Okeydokey.*

A few days later

BANNER: *How about a boat? Maybe a yacht. That's a weird word. Yacht. I had to autocorrect it.*

MY SEXY MAN: *The only boats we have any use for here are bass boats.*

BANNER: *Bass boat doesn't have the same ring to it as yacht. Shit. I spelled it wrong again! Thank you, autocorrect. If I can't spell it, I probably shouldn't own one.*

MY SEXY MAN: *Why would you want a yacht to begin with?*

BANNER: *I was watching this Discovery Channel thing on mega-yachts, and all the cool kids have them.*

MY SEXY MAN: *Do you need me to come up there and fuck the yacht thing out of you? Because you're already the coolest kid around in my book.*

BANNER: *YES, I DO. I wish you could. But I know you're busy. You're pretty cool in my book too.*

MY SEXY MAN: *Is that right?*

BANNER: *Do you need me to come down there and fuck the cool into you?*

BANNER: *That didn't quite have the same ring to it, did it?*

MY SEXY MAN: *Not quite. But I sure wish you would. Miss you, baby.*

BANNER: *Miss you more.*

A few days later

"Why'd you stop?" Logan asks.

With two fingers buried in my pussy, but unmoving, I shake my head. "Sorry. I just . . . I mean, don't take this the wrong way, but your cock has never looked bigger than it does on Skype."

Logan's gaze narrows. "Woman, you need to watch what you say. And it's clear that you need to get your ass home so you can get up close and personal again with my cock."

I laugh at his serious expression. "I'm just saying that whatever angle that is really works for you. It looks mammoth. I don't even think I could fit it in my mouth right now. If the car restoration stuff doesn't work out, you could definitely do jerk-off videos. Never mind. I didn't say that. I don't even know what those are."

"Banner . . ."

"Sorry. I just . . . I miss you so much."

Logan and I are trying to have Skype sex, and I'm so freaking happy to finally see his face (and penis) after I pestered him over and over and over again to sign up for a Skype account.

Long story short, we got naked, and I started doing my thing, Logan started doing his, and then I sort of stopped because I got so caught up in watching him do his thing.

My man *definitely* has Congo beat. By inches.

Logan drops his head back on his pillow and tosses the blanket over his lap. "I want you here. Miss you too."

I pull my hotel robe closed and reach out to touch my screen with my non-pussified fingers. "I'll be back soon. If it were up to me, I'd be done with this stuff already."

He sighs. "Do your best, Bruce. I'm gonna call it a night. I'm beat."

I want to say three words to him, especially looking at his face after two weeks apart, but I don't.

"I'll talk to you tomorrow, Logan. Sleep well."

"You too, baby."

NINE

Banner
One week later

I'M STILL IN NEW YORK, AND NOW MORE THAN EVER, I'm itching to get back to Gold Haven. Sorting out Myrna's estate has taken multiple meetings with lawyers followed by meetings with financial advisers, and then there was the never-ending packing up of her apartment and my own business to run while I did it all.

My phone rings as I flop onto the bed in my hotel room after a long freaking day finishing up with the designer who is redecorating Myrna's apartment. I don't recognize the number, but I answer it anyway because the area code is Gold Haven's.

"Hello?"

"Damn, girl. You ever planning on coming back?"

The voice is familiar, but it takes me a few seconds to place it. "Julianne?"

"Who the hell else would it be? Did you suddenly make a bunch of friends in town that I don't know about?"

"Not exactly. But I'm coming back. Hopefully really

soon."

"You might want to speed up your plans because the vultures are circling over your man. I don't know if it's because they sense he's a wounded animal, ready to be taken down, or if they're just desperate to get their last shot in before you show up again."

I stiffen. "Excuse me?"

"Gold Haven's finest are cornering him in the grocery store, and tromping in and out of his shop so often, it's a wonder the man has gotten a damn thing done."

With Julianne's vantage point from her salon across the street, I have to believe she's telling the truth.

"Bitches," I mumble under my breath.

"Definitely bitches. So I figured I'd give you the heads-up, because you know Logan, he's too damn nice to tell them to leave him the hell alone in a way they're going to take to heart."

"What do you mean?"

"The only thing Emmy Harris has ever set her sights on that she hasn't locked down is the new-and-improved Logan Brantley, and she's not backin' off without a fight. I'm pretty sure she built that house hoping he'd be moving into it with her someday soon."

Red rage fills my vision. "What the hell doesn't she understand about the word *taken*?"

"Girl, you're out of sight and out of mind for her, so you better believe she doesn't see it that way. I wanted you to know that it might be in your best interest to get your ass back here so you can stake your claim before she finds some way to snake him out from under you without him realizing it."

Even though Julianne can't see it, I prop a hand on my hip, my pose screaming WARNING: ATTITUDE AHEAD. "Logan doesn't want her. He wants me."

"But that didn't stop her from faking a pregnancy and getting a ring from the homecoming king three weeks after graduation."

"What?" Shock slams into me.

"She's a slippery bitch, and even though that didn't work out the way she planned, I wouldn't put anything past her when it comes to Logan."

"I'll be back by the end of the week."

"I wouldn't wait too long. See you soon, Banner. Oh, and can you bring me back one of those New York Fire Department T-shirts? And maybe one of those shirtless firemen too? The ones in the calendars. Wait, never mind. Firemen are assholes. Bring me an NYPD shirt and a sexy cop."

I laugh, but it sounds forced. Probably because I want to accidentally knock Emmy Harris into a ditch. With my car.

"I'll see what I can do."

After I hang up with Julianne, I tell myself I have nothing to worry about when it comes to Emmy Harris. Logan is mine. End of story.

Then why did you ask him about her bringing him dinner?

A few weeks away after even less time than that together isn't exactly the best recipe for a relationship.

And if you're not worried about Emmy Harris, why did you pay the hotel chef so much money to give you cooking classes at night?

Dammit, that little voice in my head really needs to shut up before I actually start to worry.

I know exactly what will quell it, though—I call Logan.

"Hey, Bruce. Perfect timing, I just got out of the shower."

The vision in my head is delicious. "Are you naked or wearing a towel?"

His voice deepens. "A towel, but that can change."

We've had phone sex more times than I should probably admit to over the last three weeks, and then that one hilarious attempt at Skype sex. But come on, a girl has needs, and Logan's husky drawl gets me to the finish line faster than anything else.

"Mmm, is that so? I could probably get rid of a few layers myself," I tell him.

Instead of responding with something equally sexy, Logan says, "Shit. My doorbell."

"What?"

"Someone's here."

"Should I let you go?"

I can hear his footsteps over the phone like he's headed to the door to check.

"Fuck, it's Emmy. I'll call you back, babe."

Before I can reply, Logan ends the call.

No. Fucking. Way.

Logan just answered the door to that bitch wearing only a towel?

Everything Julianne said comes back in a rush, and I bolt off the bed to grab my laptop.

It's time for me to get back to Gold Haven and *my* man.

TEN

Logan

I OPEN THE FRONT DOOR, AND EMMY'S FACE IS FLUSHED and her hair is mussed. I've never seen her this out of sorts before.

She throws herself against my bare chest and wraps her arms around my neck. My dick, semi-hard from anticipating another round of jacking off while I talk to Banner on the phone, is wedged between us awkwardly.

Jesus Christ, her timing couldn't be worse.

"I didn't know who else to come to. I'm sorry to bother you so late, but I had to talk to someone." Her words come out muffled against my shoulder.

"What's going on, Emmy? Are you okay?"

She shakes her head. "It's all too much."

I wait for a beat, hoping she's gonna explain, but she keeps holding on. I pat her shoulder and work on untangling myself from her.

Conscious of the fact that I'm only wearing a towel, I carefully unwrap her arms from around my neck and set her away from me.

Until I feel a breeze.

The buttons on Emmy's coat yanked apart my hastily tucked towel, leaving my dick swinging in the open.

I grab for the towel as it drops to the floor. I don't look up until it's wrapped around my waist and anchored firmly.

Emmy's eyes are the size of saucers, and she's not looking at my face as her hand flies up to her lips.

"Shit. Sorry. I . . . come on in. I'm gonna go throw some clothes on, and I'll be back in a second."

She steps inside, and I shut the door behind her and turn for the hall, cursing her timing every step of the way.

Fuck. Why didn't I shove her right back out the door? I take my time giving myself a mental ass-kicking as I pull on baggy sweats and a T-shirt, and return to the living room . . . to find it empty.

The clinking of dishes comes from the kitchen, and I turn to see Emmy reach up in the cupboard and bring down mugs as the scent of brewing coffee hits me.

"I know you didn't exactly say to make myself at home, but I had to keep my hands busy." She sets the mugs on the counter and rushes over to me. "I'm so sorry. I didn't mean—"

Not wanting to hear her apologize for the towel incident, or hell, do anything but forget it ever happened, I interrupt. "What's going on, Emmy?"

She wraps her arms around her body. "I'm just not used to dealing with all this. It's not normal for me."

"What happened?"

Her expression, already sober, turns more serious. "The police just interviewed me for over an hour, and I've never been so shaken up in my entire life."

58

"Cody interviewed you? About what?"

She walks back into the kitchen and fills a mug of coffee, then dumps in one packet of sugar before sliding it across the counter toward me without asking. She repeats the process with a second mug and comes around to stand beside me.

With both hands curled around the mug, she stares up, her eyes wide. "About all this drug stuff. My parents owned one of those houses that blew up. The one Roy Planter was found in."

Cody didn't mention that to me, but I'm not all that surprised.

"They own a lot of rental properties. Was he saying there was some connection to your family?"

The Harrises have always been one of the richest families in the county, and only partly due to the success of Home Cookin'. They own a square mile or so out near the county line where they have their compound, a few cabins, and Emmy's new house that she's been building for over a year.

Emmy's voice is weak as she continues. "He didn't straight-out say there was a connection, but he implied it strongly. And then there were more questions that just scared the daylights out of me."

"Like what?"

"About a couple of my employees they suspect might be either using or buying stuff to make the drugs. He wanted to know if I knew of anyone else who seemed suspicious."

"What did you tell him?"

"That we can't be a unified town if we're going to be looking at our neighbors like they're suspects. Then we'll all be at each other's throats instead of working together to try to put an end to this."

I actually agree with Emmy's sentiment. I hate to look at the people coming into my shop and wonder who's dealing and who's buying or supplying.

"What did Cody say to that?"

"If we want our town back, I need to be more vigilant in watching my customers and people from out of town who seem out of place."

When she mentions people from out of town, I immediately think of Banner. Apparently, so does Emmy.

"Cody thought it was quite the coincidence that nothing else has happened since your friend left to go back to New York."

Anger rises up from the depths of my gut. "Banner doesn't have shit to do with any of this. The first house exploded before she even got here."

Emmy looks up at me, an expression of pure innocence on her face, but there's no way it's genuine. "That's exactly what I told him."

She pauses and sips her coffee, still gripping the mug as though it's keeping her together. When she finally meets my gaze again, the innocent expression has faded.

"I'm not going to pretend that I like her, Logan. I'm not going to pretend that I'm not upset you've picked her over me when you knew I was building my house for both of us. But I guess my small-town upbringing isn't good enough for you anymore."

Emmy's honesty surprises me, as does the comment about her house. *I fucked up by not putting that idea out of her head.*

But her accusation about not being good enough pisses me off. Emmy Harris was always the princess who sat on the pedestal above everyone else and got whatever she wanted. Maybe that's why I didn't shut her down hard. Maybe I liked that Emmy Harris, who wouldn't have talked to me as a teenager, finally found me worthy.

It wasn't until Banner came into my life that the chip on my shoulder started shrinking. Still, the time has come to set Emmy straight.

"I'm gonna be plain with you, Emmy. That last bit is bullshit, and we both know it. I spent so many years not being worthy of anyone in this town, I'm the last person who's going to pretend like Gold Haven or anyone from here isn't good enough for me."

Her shoulders straighten. "So you just like her better than me. I get it. I built the fairy tale in my head, but apparently I didn't take into account the fact that the prince would fall for someone else. I know when I've lost. You don't have to tell me again."

The fact that she says *lost* like I'm some kind of prize pisses me off, but it doesn't matter. All I want is to get Emmy out of my kitchen so I can call Banner back. I can already imagine how well that conversation will go.

Emmy takes another sip of her coffee before sitting it on the counter. "I hope we can still be friends, Logan. I would hate to think you being with her would change that."

If it gets her out of my kitchen faster, I can give her that reassurance. "Of course."

She smiles again, but it wobbles. "I guess I should get going. I just . . . I didn't know who else to talk to about this whole mess. I can't believe we even have to deal with it. This isn't the town I remember anymore."

I nod. "That's the truth."

Emmy steps away from the counter. "Sorry to interrupt your night." She heads for the door, but pauses on the threshold. "There was one other question Cody asked that threw me for a loop, and I'm not sure what to make of it."

"What?"

"He asked me if I knew anything about Nicole, or how she's raising money to buy Pints and Pins from Ben."

I jerk my head back. "What?"

"That was my reaction too. I told him I don't know her well at all, but we all know she's dead set on owning that bowling alley, and hustles every minute of every day so she can make it happen. I've always admired her drive in that respect. She rents a cabin on my parents' land, so my first thought was whether or not I need to walk around and see if she's got her own meth lab going."

"Is that what you told Cody?"

Emmy shakes her head. "No, I didn't want to point fingers. I can't imagine she would, you know?"

The memory of Nicole trying and failing to buy something from the pharmacy the night Banner and I went on a hunt for lube flashes through my mind. *No fucking way is she making meth. I don't believe it.* But it doesn't add up.

"I've known Nicole a long time, and I can't see her stooping that low to make a buck."

Emmy nods. "I agree. It just struck me as odd, that's all. I'll let you get back to your evening. Sorry for bothering you, Logan. I hope Banner realizes what a good guy she's got. Because if she doesn't . . ." Emmy trails off, but her point is clear.

It's also a statement I won't touch with a ten-foot pole. "Good night. Drive safe."

She opens the door and steps out. I close it and lock it behind her, my thoughts going in a dozen different directions.

Part of me wants to go right over to Pints and Pins and talk to Nicole, but it's not my job or my business. On the other hand, we're friends, and I've been looking out for her a long time.

How is she making extra money? She works her shifts at the factory and the bowling alley, but it's been at least six weeks since she's pulled a shift at the shop doing oil changes.

Fuck, I hate that I'm even thinking about this.

I grab my phone and call Banner back, fully expecting an earful about me answering the door to Emmy Harris wearing only a towel.

Instead, I get Banner's voice mail.

"No one leaves voice mails anymore. Text me if it's important. And if you're trying to sell me something, go buy a bag of dicks."

I leave a message anyway. "Bruce, call me back."

I'm still trying to keep my eyes open after two hours of watching *SportsCenter*, but my phone doesn't ring before I fall into bed.

ELEVEN

Banner

ONE BRILLIANT THING ABOUT NEW YORK? Everything is open late, and that worked perfectly for my defensive shopping last night.

When I walk onto the plane taking me to Gold Haven, I've got one more suitcase than I left with, packed with enough scandalous lingerie to destroy any man's inhibitions.

Do I think I really need it to make sure I have no competition for Logan?

Of course not. Don't be ridiculous. I'm fucking fabulous, and that man is lucky to have me.

I remind myself of that no fewer than eighty times on the flight. But that doesn't mean I'm about to leave anything to chance.

Also with me—more lube. Just in case.

Brown Town, here we come.

I'm a woman on a mission when I step off my last flight at six o'clock at night, annoyed it took me an entire freaking day to get here since I made my plans at the last minute. As soon as I leave the rental car desk, I'm headed for my first destination. Logan's shop.

He's never going to know what hit him. My skirt is short, my heels are tall, and my hair, skin, and nails are perfect from the pampering I managed to sneak in this week.

I pull into the parking lot an hour and a half later, mostly because I was so busy singing along to every kick-ass female anthem on my playlist that I missed the turn and went fifteen miles in the wrong direction.

But no one needs to know that little detail.

The lights are still on, and Logan's truck is parked in its normal spot alongside the building. No other cars remain in the lot.

I pull out my phone and switch it out of airplane mode. I told myself I kept it there all day because I was worried about the safety of my flights and obviously because of the FAA regulations, but that's total bull.

I didn't trust myself not to answer what must be at least a few messages from Logan. I wanted this to be a surprise. Like when Logan thought I might be pregnant, this is a discussion that needs to happen in person.

A few text messages pop up from him immediately, and they're progressively more . . . let's call it assertive.

MY SEXY MAN: *Bruce, call me.*

MY SEXY MAN: *Seriously, babe. Call me.*

MY SEXY MAN: *CALL ME.*

MY SEXY MAN: *This radio silence shit will not fly. Call me, Bruce.*

MY SEXY MAN: *Banner Regent, don't even try to dodge me. I know where you are, and I will come to you and show you how a real man handles this situation.*

A smile spreads over my face. I've come to terms with a few things in the last twenty-four hours, and one of them is that I don't care if I'm the first one to say those words I've been holding back. I love Logan Brantley, and I'm not going to let another day go by without telling him. To his face.

After I park, I slide out of the car, careful not to pull a Britney and flash anyone my vag because I'm going commando under this skirt, and strut my ass up to the entrance.

I push on the door that opens into the waiting room, but it doesn't budge. Locked. Well, dammit, that's not part of my plan. I bang on it, but no one comes. The beat of whatever rock song he's listening to is thumping through the walls.

I pull my phone out of my wristlet and text him back.

BANNER: *Open the damn door.*

A response pops up in seconds.

MY SEXY MAN: *What door?*
BANNER: *I'm waiting.*

That's when the music volume drops and I get my first real look at Logan after three weeks. Damn, he's sexy, especially when he's angry.

He's still wiping his dripping hands on a rag and shoving it into his pocket when he stalks into the waiting room to twist the lock and yank the door open.

"The next time you wait twenty-four hours to answer me and have me thinking all the awful fucking things that could've happened to you in New York, I swear I will put you over my lap and spank some goddamned sense into you."

I should probably be annoyed, but his threat turns me on more than anything. I'm also not about to let him forget how this whole situation came about.

"Maybe, just maybe, you might want to think twice the next time you answer your door in a towel to a woman who wants your dick."

"I wouldn't give a single fuck if she showed up naked at my door on her knees. The only woman I want is you."

Lust and adrenaline burn through my veins as I smile. "I know."

His eyes widen a fraction. "What do you mean, you know?"

"If you feel half of what I'm feeling, then you're so in love with me, you wouldn't notice if she twerked on your dick in the middle of church."

"You're in love with me." The words come out slow and measured.

"You're the best man I've ever met, Logan Brantley. Of course I am."

He pulls me inside and locks the door behind me. Heat burns in his gaze. "Say it."

"I love you."

Logan's lips crush down on mine before I'm finished speaking them, and he pours every bit of emotion running through him into me.

I pull my head back. "Now, you say it."

"I fucking love you, Banner."

He lifts me up, and my legs wrap around his waist instinctively.

"I brought the lube," I whisper as he carries me into the shop and sets me on the unfinished hood of a car.

"You're going to kill me, woman."

"Only in the best way possible."

TWELVE

Logan

BANNER UNWRAPS HER ARMS FROM AROUND MY NECK, scoots up, and lies back on the unpainted hood of Boone Thrasher's Olds 442. Somehow, her red lips are still intact, even though I kissed the hell out of her. God, she's so fucking beautiful with that sexy smile and her hair spread out everywhere. The strap of her little purse is still wrapped around her wrist.

"You managed to fit lube in that little thing?"

Her smile widens. "Packets. A bunch of them. TSA wouldn't let me bring the supersized bottle through security. I tried to slip it in . . ."

Just like it has from the beginning, Banner's humor never fails to make me laugh. The sound booms out through the garage, over the AC/DC I'd picked for tonight.

"I can't even imagine what you must have said to them."

Banner untwines her legs from around my waist before spreading them and placing each foot on the hood.

Holy. Fucking. Shit.

I can see straight up her skirt and into the best vision of

heaven I've ever known.

One hand, tipped with blood-red nails that match her heels, slides down to her bare thigh. Her voice goes husky. "I told them I was going to make someone a very happy man, so denying me my lube was denying one of their brothers a very fine piece of ass."

I wrap a hand around each of her thighs and yank her back down to me. "Is that right?"

"I thought they'd understand since I was planning to take one for the team, but no dice."

"You probably had all their dicks hard as they watched you walk away."

"They were poppin' chubs before I even zipped my bag."

A growl is unleashed from my throat as my possessive instincts fire up. "My. Pie. I don't share my pie with anyone. Thought we had an understanding, Bruce."

"You better remind me. It's been a while since you showed me what it means to be yours."

Always a challenge. This woman will never be boring.

I loosen my grip on her thighs and slide both palms up her smooth skin, rucking up the material of her short skirt as I go. "You better not have bent over in this thing, or else I'm gonna have to go find whoever saw this sweet little cunt and make sure they understand who it belongs to."

Her whiskey eyes flame.

"You love it when I say that." I cover her bare pussy with my hand. It's not a question. Her body tells me everything I need to know. I keep my gaze pinned to hers as I trail a finger down her soaked slit. "Dripping for me. Sweet heaven." Dragging my index finger around her clit, I watch as her pupils dilate with need. My cock, already hard as tempered steel, pulses at her responsiveness.

"I'm going to fuck you on the hood of this car. First your tight little pussy, and then I'm going to bend you over and take that sweet ass you've been teasing me with for weeks."

Banner's teeth close over her bottom lip as her hips lift to increase the pressure from my fingers on her clit, but she doesn't answer.

I pull my hand back two inches and plunge a finger inside her.

Banner sucks in a breath and arches off the hood. I add a second finger, and fuck them in and out of her until the word I love to hear falls from her lips.

"Please."

"Anything for you. Any-fucking-thing."

I shove down my jeans with my free hand, letting my cock spring free.

Banner reaches out as though she wants to touch my dick, but I stop her. "Hands on the hood. I'm calling the shots here. You might not be naked, but you're still gonna do what you're told."

Her pussy contracts around my fingers in response.

I fucking love this woman.

Her hands land palm down on the hood just before a horn honks outside, probably at the Four Corners, trying to get someone to drive through the blinking red signal.

Banner's gaze cuts to the high windows in the overhead door where anyone could see us if they were looking, especially with all the lights on inside here.

I wait for her to say something about moving, but she doesn't. Her pussy grows even wetter.

"Someone could see us. Watch me fuck you on the hood of this car. What do you think about that, Banner?"

Her lips curl up in a dead sexy smile. "We better give them a hell of a show."

I pull my fingers free of her heat and line my dick up with her entrance before gripping her hips with both hands.

"That's a guarantee." I pull her toward me as I push inside, sinking balls deep with one thrust. "*Fuuuck*." I throw my head back as I yell it out.

Banner arches into it, her fingers curling into fists. "It's been way too long." Her words come out on a rush of breath.

"I'm not doing this shit again, Banner. Not waitin' three weeks to get inside this pussy. Ain't happening. I want you every day."

THIRTEEN

Banner

BEFORE I CAN RESPOND TO LOGAN'S WORDS, HE pulls back and slams into me. My hips lift off the hood of the car, meeting his every thrust. This isn't just a fuck; this is a claiming. I've never seen the look of possession in anyone's eyes before, but I recognize it in Logan's.

For the first time in my life, I'm happy to be possessed.

He owns me, and not just my body.

Pleasure zings through me, forming into an overwhelming wave that needs only the slightest push to take me over the edge. My fingers flex and clench over and over, and I want to touch my clit and steal my orgasm, but Logan told me to keep them where they are and I'm determined to follow that order.

As though he can tell I need it, Logan releases one hand from my waist and presses his thumb against my clit.

Instant explosion.

My hips lift again of their own accord, and I scream his name.

"Yes, oh my God. Yes."

Logan's hooded gaze flashes as he pulls out. I miss the fullness immediately, but I know what's coming next, and my entire body is ready.

He reaches for my wristlet, and I unfist my hand to let him slide it off. He looks down and unzips it before pulling out a half dozen packets of lube.

"I fucking love you, Banner."

A smile slides over my lips. "You're just saying that because I'm gonna let you put it in my butt."

He shakes his head. "No, I'm saying it because it's the goddamned truth." He drops my wristlet on the hood of the car and lays the packets on top of it. Logan holds out a hand, and I lean up to take it as he helps me down from the hood.

"I hope I didn't scratch—"

"Doesn't fucking matter."

He cups my face between both hands and covers my lips with his for only a moment before pulling back. With his eyes on mine, he says, "Turn around and bend over. Now that we've practiced, I know you can keep your hands on the hood like a good girl."

The command sends bolts of lust shooting through me. "You're so sexy when you're telling me how you're going to fuck me."

His eyes blaze. "We haven't even gotten that far yet. Now, do it."

I bite down on my lip, and I'm pretty sure the slickness from my pussy is slipping down my thighs. I turn and bend over, feeling everything with heightened intensity. The warmth of the roughened metal where my body was pressed to it only moments ago. The smooth patches where I lay my hands. The burning heat of Logan's palm where it lands on the small of my back and presses me down further before catching the bottom hem of the back of my skirt and dragging it up over my ass. The cool air that hits my skin as his growl of approval reaches me.

"Spread your feet."

I follow directions, but apparently not well enough.

"Wider, and tilt your hips up. I want to see that little pink pussy I just fucked."

Sliding my heels another few inches apart, I lift my ass and cant my hips. Jesus Christ, if anyone sees this from the windows I was riveted on before, they're going to get an eyeful. Of all of me.

I couldn't care less. All that matters is where Logan is going to touch me, and how hard he's going to make me come.

The palm of his hand lands between my legs, slapping my pussy. I suck in a breath as a shaft of pleasure zips from my clit to my nipples.

"Wider and higher," he growls.

I do as he says, now feeling obscene in my position, but Logan thinks it's just perfect.

"Sweet fucking Christ. If you could see yourself right now . . ."

I picture how I must look to him, and I'm not ashamed of what I see in my head. From my peripheral vision, I see Logan grab one of the packets. He must tear it open because moments later, the cold, slippery gel lands on my ass. Logan smooths it around the pucker, lighting up nerve endings that haven't seen action in a while.

Part of me wishes that I'd never done this before so I could give Logan at least one first, but then I remind myself it's a good thing it's not the first time, what with the monster he's packing in his pants. I gave him the most important first, anyway—my heart.

My brain goes momentarily blank when Logan presses a finger inside.

I don't know what it is about the back door, but every time seems to *feel* like the first time. And regardless of how I've made it sound over the years to my best friend, my ass is the closest thing I have to virgin territory.

"You're so damned tight."

He adds more lube as he goes, and then . . . Holy. Jesus. A second finger. I press back as he pushes inside.

"Holy shit. Your fingers feel way bigger than I thought."

He scissors them apart, twisting and stretching me. When he pulls them out, I hear another package tearing open, and I picture Logan lubing up his cock, and all those nerve endings he just lit up spark and tense when I think about how big he's going to feel.

Logan leans forward over my body and speaks into my ear as the thick head of his cock presses against my ass. "You're gonna strangle my cock, but you won't keep me out. This ass is mine tonight, and you're gonna beg me to fuck it again and again because you're about to come harder than you ever have before."

Sweet hell, I think I'm already about to come and he hasn't even breached—and then he does.

I hold my breath as inch by body-shaking inch, Logan sinks his cock deep inside me. When I feel his balls against my pussy, I blow out.

76

"How're you doing, baby? Can you handle me?"

I press back against him, taking him another fraction of an inch. "I can take everything you want to give me."

Logan groans, and his chest vibrates against my back. "I know you can."

My pussy drips down my legs, and again, I want to touch myself, but I'm following orders.

Logan seems to have figured out the tricks to my body because he reaches around with his left hand and covers my clit with his fingers, pressing, strumming, and circling as he fucks my ass with smooth strokes increasing in speed with every thrust.

FOURTEEN

Logan

BANNER'S ORGASM CATCHES ME OFF GUARD. HER body tightens, and my name echoes off the wall of my shop along with her cries. It's the most beautiful sound I've ever heard, after her telling me she loved me for the first time.

This woman could wreck me, but I'm going to enjoy the inferno.

I keep up my thrusts, increasing the pace and pressure on her clit, and I can't tell if she starts coming again or just never quit.

Broken words and pleas fall from her lips, but so long as every one of them is pleasure, I'm not stopping.

My orgasm boils up in my balls, preparing to shoot down my spine like a bolt of lightning that will end me. With one final cry from Banner, I lose my grip on control and my body tenses, spilling inside her.

"*Fuuucking love you.*"

I fall forward, catching myself with both palms on the hood, sucking in oxygen like I just remembered how to breathe.

"Holy hell. I think . . . I don't know. I . . ." Banner's disjointed words trail off.

"What, baby?"

"I don't know if that's the longest orgasm I've ever had . . . or the most. I don't know. Either way, I win."

I press a kiss to the top of her shoulder. "I think we both won, Bruce."

Pulling away, I sidestep and rip some clean shop towels off the roll, then snag a bottle of water to clean us both up with.

Banner flops over on her back, her arms spread even wider than her smile.

"So, who's going to tell Boone Thrasher his car has already been to Brown Town?"

FIFTEEN

Banner

WALKING INTO PINTS AND PINS THE NEXT night with Logan's hand on the small of my back gives me a sense of belonging I didn't have the last time I came here. The bowling alley is packed with people, and almost all the tables in the bar area are taken.

"What's the occasion?" I ask him.

"Pay-per-view fight. None of the other places around get it, and most people don't want to shell out fifty bucks or more to watch. Ben takes donations at the bar rather than charging an entry fee, and it usually covers the cost. Plus, he makes it up in alcohol and food sales."

I scan the crowded room as I nod. It makes sense, even though it's not something I would have ever guessed in my limited knowledge of what makes people gather in bowling alleys. The women are dressed in their country finest—jeans with silver stitching and rhinestones on the back pockets, fringed leather purses, fancy cowboy boots, and tight tops with plunging necklines.

Several of them light up when they see Logan, but their expressions turn to disappointment as soon as they realize I'm standing next to him.

Damn, I guess Julianne was right. The vultures are circling. I need to thank her for the call more than I realized. I understand the disappointment I'm seeing on a few faces, because if I lost out on my shot with Logan, I'd be devastated too.

Their judging eyes take in my outfit from the toes of my shiny Louboutin boots, up my skinny jeans, my sexy-but-casual black tunic-length tee, and my fan-freaking-tastic statement necklace—one of the few splurges I made with my new inheritance. The Swarovski crystals, black onyx, and gold catch the light and draw attention to my throat.

Julianne, just the woman I wanted to see, struts toward Logan and me with a drink in her hand and a man trailing behind her.

"Hey, city girl. Thought you'd bolted out of here for good. I would say I don't have any idea why you'd bother to come back, but I do. By the way, if the vultures shred you to pieces, can I have the necklace?"

Logan wraps an arm around my shoulders. His tone is no-nonsense. "Of course she came back. And no one is going to say anything to Banner while I'm around." He doesn't acknowledge the man with Julianne, which surprises me.

Julianne laughs. "Maybe, maybe not. But they'll definitely have plenty to say as soon as you're not connected at the hip."

I straighten my shoulders. "Hey, I can handle myself. I'm a big girl."

"You tell me if anyone says a cross word, and I'll deal with it," Logan says.

With a sweet smile, I reply, "There won't be anything to handle. I'll be fine." I look back to Julianne. "Who's your friend?"

The man reaches out a hand to Logan. "Good to see you again, Brantley."

"Mitch." Logan's tone is curt, and he doesn't shake the man's hand.

"Come on, boys, it was a long time ago. Besides, Logan, you're the one who kicked Mitch's ass."

"No hard feelings, man," Mitch says, lifting both hands into the air.

My gaze is darting back and forth between Mitch and Logan like I'm watching a Ping-Pong match, which I'd never actually do. With the exception of *Forrest Gump*, I guess.

"What am I missing?" I ask when I realize no one is going to fill me in, and the awkward silence grows too heavy for what's supposed to be a fun night out for Logan and me.

"Mitch here thought it was his job to beat my ass when he found out I took his sister on a date."

"Excuse me?" I prop my hands on my hips.

"It was years ago, city. Calm your tits," Julianne says.

"Some things take a hell of a lot longer to forget." Logan's words come out low.

"Look, man. I'm sorry." Mitch shoves his hands in his pockets. "Would it make you feel better if I told you I'd rather you knocked her up than that piece of shit she married a year after she graduated? He's a drunk. Hardly leaves his fucking chair in their living room while he spends all the money she makes working part-time at the pharmacy on porn and guns. Fuck, I wish I'd shoved her into your car rather than pulled her out, because her life would be a hell of a lot better than the one she's got now."

The tense set of Logan's shoulders eases by a few degrees. "I'm sorry she's having such a rough time. I didn't realize."

Mitch shakes his head. "She doesn't tell anyone. She's too embarrassed. I've been trying to get her to leave him for years, but she just keeps going to church and saying that she'll find a way to carry the burden herself."

"I even tried to talk to her about it when she was in the salon," Julianne says. "But she doesn't wanna hear nothin' from nobody."

"That's so sad." I don't mean to say it out loud, but everyone looks at me and Mitch nods soberly.

"Sure isn't what I wanted for my little sister."

Julianne leans into him, and Mitch wraps his arm around her shoulders.

Logan holds out his hand to the man. "I'm good with burying the hatchet. I think you've beat yourself up more than I ever could."

The men shake hands.

"Can I at least buy you a beer?" Mitch offers.

Logan glances down at me. "You want to go order some food at the window, and I'll get us some drinks and find a table?"

I look at the line of people at the food window and the three-deep crowd around the bar. "Sure. What do you want?"

"Cheeseburger. Medium. Everything on it, and a basket of fries."

"Sure."

I take one step away from him, but his arm tightens around me. "You forgetting something?"

Confused, I meet his gaze. "No?"

Logan releases his hold and lifts his hand to my chin to tilt it up before pressing a kiss to my lips. His blue eyes flash, and I strongly suspect this is Logan's way of staking his claim in front of the crowd of people.

"You two are so damn cute together," Julianne says before she and Mitch slide into the crowd with Logan behind them.

I turn toward the food line, but I can't help looking over my shoulder. Halfway to the bar, Logan has stopped and is shaking hands with another guy, doing that thing where guys lean back on their heels and talk to each other.

I move sideways a little to get a better look at him, but someone bumps into my shoulder.

"Watch your step."

Jerking my head up, I open my mouth to apologize, but I snap the words back before they can leave my throat. It's the blonde who was talking shit about me to her little crew of friends in the aisle at Piggly Wiggly when I first came to town. The one I boldly informed that Logan had already found my clit, my G-spot, and the back of my throat.

"Excuse me?"

"I said you better watch your step, you little city bitch."

Well, that's uncalled for and just plain rude. "Maybe you should watch your mouth." I pitch my suggestion as politely as possible.

"Why? You afraid Logan is going to slide his dick in it and forget you exist? I bet he'd have trouble finding the back of my throat when I can take him *all the way down*."

"Seriously? Did you just brag about your deep-throating skills in a bowling alley? Wow."

Reeling with how to respond, I survey her from head to toe. Bleached-blond hair with a half inch of dark roots desperately needing attention, tight pink shirt that does nothing for her figure, and even tighter black jeans that are riding low and accentuating her muffin top.

"What are you going to do about it?"

"Suggest you get those roots taken care of so you can find your own man instead of wishing you could have mine."

The man in front of me in line, approximately the size of a grizzly bear, turns around with interest at our conversation. "Shit, if this is gonna turn into a catfight, can we take it outside so more people can watch? I'd put my money on you, sweetheart." He's looking at me, and his vote of confidence is somehow kind, but the suggestion that we're actually going to fight is ridiculous.

"Shut up, Stan. I'd whup her ass and rip those extensions right out of her head."

That actually makes me laugh. "Oh, honey. You're so misguided that you can't tell real hair from extensions. Just because you have them doesn't mean everyone else does. What is it you say down here? *Bless your heart*?"

"Buuurn, Tricia," Stan says, doing a fair impression of Ashton Kutcher from his *That 70s Show* days.

"Shut up, Stan. You stay out of this."

Stan shakes his head. "Fuck no. This could be better than the real fights. Lemme get some popcorn out of the machine. I'll be right back. Don't start without me."

When Stan lumbers off, I move up in line, hoping I can turn around and Tricia will walk away, but the two other men ahead of me are facing us, watching the exchange. Tricia's shoulders stiffen, and I have a feeling her pride is on the line.

"Why don't you just go back to where you came from? Aren't there ten million men in New York or something?"

I laugh. "Not exactly, and I'm not leaving."

"You probably slept with every single one of them, and they all know what a skank ho you are now so you had to run a thousand miles away to start over. Women like you are the ones who give all of us a bad name."

"You might want to stop, because you sound ridiculous."

She pushes out her tits and crosses her arms under them. "We'll run you out of town if we have to. Don't think we won't."

I assume she's talking about her little grocery store posse, but she doesn't realize that they just make me more determined to stay. "You can try."

"Boys, are you gonna order or what?"

The two men standing between the food window and me are watching us like idiots, so I take my turn and step between them. I don't need to deal with bad roots and an even worse attitude tonight. I'm here with Logan, and life is good.

"I've got an order to place. Two cheeseburgers, medium, with everything on them, and a giant basket of fries."

The girl, who doesn't look any older than sixteen, scribbles it down wide-eyed. She definitely caught at least part of the exchange with Blondie McRoots. "Is there anything else I can get you?"

"That's all. Thank you so much."

She gives me a total and I slide the cash toward her. "Keep the change."

"Thank you." She hands me a red plastic number with a smile. "We'll bring it out when it's ready."

I thank her again and turn more carefully this time. Sure enough, Tricia and the two guys are still standing there, waiting for who knows what, and Stan is hurrying back with a basket of popcorn, shoving a handful in his mouth with nearly every step.

"You girls ready to take this outside? We've already got takers for bets!"

I give him a pointed look. "I think you're mistaken. I don't fight in bowling alley parking lots, or any other parking lots, for that matter."

Tricia's face twists into an angry mask. "You're too good for that, huh? I should've figured, what with you being a cuntbag who won't be able to keep her man."

I cross my arms, the red plastic number gripped tightly between my fingers. "You're really gonna go there? Just throwing out the C-word? Are bar fights something you do for fun on the weekends?"

"Slut," she spits at me.

I look up at the ceiling like maybe it'll stop me from doing something I'll regret. *Like that has ever worked.* I send a quick little ditty up to the big man anyway.

Dear Lord, please stop me from knocking out this girl's teeth because I'll probably have to buy her veneers, and I'll be pissed because her teeth will look better than mine. Amen.

Sucking in a deep breath, I meet Tricia's hate-filled gaze again.

"You're just a piece of ass to him. When he's done, he'll send you crawling home on your knees, although that's probably how you're used to spending your time."

Damn, she's really trying to piss me off, and now . . . she's succeeding. My temper flares, and the crowd around us grows.

"You must think you need to save face in a big way right now, because you've got no skin in this game, Tricia. Seriously, back off. I don't give a shit what you say to me—"

"I bet you'd give a shit if Logan Brantley buried himself balls-deep in Emmy Harris's ass. You're just a warm-up for what he really wants."

That's it. I'm *done* playing nice.

"Go fuck yourself, or better yet, go fuck your inbred hick brother."

Her mouth drops open, and I must have hit a nerve because she launches herself at me with a battle cry.

"Don't you dare talk about my brother. My mama didn't know!"

The words don't even compute in my head—beyond *what in the ever-loving fuck*—before her fist flies toward my face.

Pain from the glancing blow shoots through my cheekbone as I stumble backward, knocked off my feet. Another stab of pain screams up my spine as my tailbone connects with the hard floor of the bowling alley.

All of a sudden, Tricia is on top of me, and I hear Stan yelling, "Girl fight! *Live* at Pints and Pins!" in his best impression of that Buffer guy who's always getting people ready to rumble.

I raise my hands, trying to protect my face, wishing I'd

joined the jujitsu craze at my gym a few years ago. Tricia tries to slap me, but I throw my elbow up to block. And damn, she's a hell of a lot heavier than she looks because she's like dead weight on top of me.

Everyone's yelling, and I'm just trying to cover up—until she reaches for my brand-new necklace.

Oh, fuck no, bitch. That's my Swarovski splurge. I grab her wrist and twist it until she screams, and someone lifts her off me.

"Did you see what she did? That bitch! She assaulted me." Tricia's screech cuts through the rising sound of the crowd around us.

Someone touches my shoulder, and I lash out before I hear Logan's deep drawl.

"Whoa, Bruce. It's me. You okay?" Logan's face is a picture of fury.

I start to nod, but pain coming from my cheek and my ass and the back of my head brings tears to my eyes. *Dammit, I will not cry in front of these people.*

"Shit. You're not okay."

"I'm fine." I sniffle and bite my lip. "It just hurts a little. She's heavier than she looks."

Another person crouches down next to me. Nicole. "And she's already had three Jack and Cokes and was talking shit about you before you got here. I swear, the chip on her shoulder hasn't shrunk since high school. You want me to go kick her ass for you, since Logan here is too good of a guy to ever lay a hand on a woman?"

Logan growls something, but my head is pounding too loudly for me to make out his alpha-speak right now.

"I just want to go home."

"Y'all get back to your seats. Nothing to see here," Ben croaks out as he shuffles toward us, leaning on his cane. "Shit, please tell me she didn't hurt you. If you sue me, I'll lose everything."

Logan helps me to my feet, and I face the old man.

"It's not your fault. I should've walked away."

When he holds out a white bag, I stare at it, unmoving.

"I don't have frozen peas or a steak, but here's some frozen tater tots you can hold on your face for a little bit. Shit, you can even keep 'em for a snack later if you want. On me."

I would have said nothing could make me laugh at that moment, but Ben proves me wrong.

My entire body shakes, and Logan stiffens, pulling me against his chest in a hug. "Baby, don't cry. I'm so fucking sorry I brought you here tonight."

But I can't help it. It bursts from my lips and I laugh so hard, tears run down my face.

SIXTEEN

Logan

I T TAKES EVERY BIT OF RESTRAINT IN MY BODY NOT TO send Nicole after Tricia. That woman has started more fights in this town than the rest of the females put together, I swear. And for some reason, when I came back after I left the corps, she was one who set her sights on me, right along with Emmy Harris and the others.

I know it's because she's goddamned miserable, sorting and delivering mail after her husband got promoted at the furniture factory and then left town with his secretary. Tricia used to be a stay-at-home mom before, and now she looks real hard at any man who can give her back the lifestyle she lost. But that doesn't mean she gets a free pass to take a swing at my woman, and regardless of everything I know, I don't have an ounce of sympathy for her situation anymore.

When I heard the yelling, I knew in my gut Banner was probably involved. I've made her a target in this town, and I have to find some way to reset the situation or I'll never be able to talk her into staying long term. That's right,

Logan Brantley, Gold Haven's King of No Commitment, wants to settle down, and I'll be goddamned if I'll let some small-minded assholes get in the way. There are plenty of kind folks here, and that's who Banner needs to be around. Not the spiteful and bitter ones like Tricia.

I push open the door and we step outside into the parking lot. Banner pauses, so I do as well.

"Something wrong, Bruce?"

She looks fucking adorable with the bag of frozen tater tots pressed to her face. I swear, no one else could manage to look beautiful right now except Banner.

"I'm sorry. She said some stuff. I said some stuff. Her stuff was way worse than mine, though. I could've gotten downright nasty, but I was holding myself back because I don't want to make you look bad for being with me. I didn't have a clue her brother was really inbred. Seriously. What are the odds?"

I wrap a hand around each of her shoulders. "You could never make me look bad. Never. If not knowing who my dad is, and having my ma OD in her own living room hasn't stopped me from making a living in this town, there's nothing you could do. So don't ever worry about it."

She lowers the tater tots from her face. "I love you, Logan. But I think I just complicate your life."

I open my mouth to respond that's the most ridiculous thing I've ever heard, and she's the best complication I've ever had in my life, but two slamming car doors interrupt.

"Well, well. Looks like we missed the real entertainment," Rusty Mills says as gravel crunches under his boots. But that's not what surprises me; it's the woman following him.

Emmy Harris.

Jesus, she could at least have found a better substitute for me than some guy who's going to try to drain her of all her cash, because everyone knows he's living on disability for an injury he doesn't even have.

Banner tries to tuck the tater tots out of sight, but she's not quick enough.

"Oh no, what happened? Did you fall?" Emmy asks.

"Looks like your girl lost a fight, Brantley."

The door to the bowling alley bursts open behind us and Stan comes out, yellow streaks on his shirt from the popcorn seasoning. "Did I miss it?"

"Go back inside, Stan."

"But they threw Tricia out for fighting, and I figure she's waiting in the parking lot to jump y'all like she tried with . . ." He trails off when he sees Emmy. "Uh, I guess I don't have to tell you what happened, Emmy."

Emmy's face turns red. "That woman is a menace. If I wasn't carrying that day, who knows what she would've tried to do to me."

I look from Emmy to Stan and back. "Are you saying that Tricia came after you too?"

"You didn't know? Shit, dude. I thought I was the last to find out everything in this town. Apparently not."

Fuck, now guilt is creeping in because apparently that crazy chick has gone after two women connected with me. "Anything else I need to know, Stan? Emmy? Because, what the fuck?"

Emmy hugs her purse tighter to her side. "I took care of myself." She shoots a look at Banner. "I didn't need any rumors spreading around town about me. I have a business to run and a reputation to uphold. Besides, smart girls in the country carry guns."

Banner stiffens beside me and puts a hand on my arm. "I guess you're going to have to teach me how to shoot, Logan. Because apparently I'm not well enough equipped to live here and deal with Kentucky women without one."

I hate that she has to say something like that. I'm also more than a little concerned about the idea of Banner carrying a gun.

Rusty's grating laugh rings out, and I want to knock that fucker down a few notches. "Who knew you could find a high-class bitch who'd fit in with us poor country folk so well."

When he says the word *bitch*, everything in me goes still.

"You better shut your mouth, Rusty, or I'll gladly shut it for you."

The man, who doesn't have balls nearly as big as he pretends, shuts up quick.

"We're just here to watch the fights."

"So maybe you should get on inside and do that. Let's get out of here." I wrap an arm around Banner, who now apparently doesn't care who sees her holding tater tots to her face, and we head toward my truck.

Once inside, I hear another engine start. It's not until I'm backing out of the full parking lot that I see headlights flip on at the end of the row.

It's Tricia's old Buick.

SEVENTEEN

Logan

"**D**ID YOU HEAR ABOUT THAT REPORTER WHO checked into the Sleep Over this morning? I was over at Home Cookin' for some grub before I came in, and word is that there really is some national news chick here to investigate this whole meth story. Wonder if there'll be more coming?"

Jock leans against Lonnie's Camaro that we've stopped working on because Lonnie won't approve the estimated repairs. Apparently he doesn't have the cash to float the project like he thought he did when he dropped it off, but he doesn't seem to be in a hurry to pick it up either.

The reporter story Jock is feeding me is definitely news. "Is that right?"

Jock sips his coffee and nods. "Heard she's real cute too. Maybe she'll come over here to do some interviews, and we can get a look at her."

I cross over to the toolbox to grab a different size socket, and turn back to him. "We don't have time for interviews. We've gotta get Boone Thrasher's car in perfect condition in less than two weeks, or I'm going to lose the biggest opportunity I've ever had."

His expression cowed, Jock lowers his mug. "I'm just making conversation, man. I thought it was interesting. I heard that Chief Timmons is actually trying to figure some shit out now instead of sitting around with his thumb up his ass."

My irritation slides away at his explanation, because it's the truth. "You're right, but I'm starting to feel this deadline breathing down my neck, and now Mrs. Borst isn't answering her phone so I can get an update on the interior panels and upholstery. We gotta have this car ready for paint by next week."

He nods. "I know, Logan. We'll get it done. We're all puttin' in the time." He pauses as he walks to his workbench to set down his mug. "Isn't Mrs. Borst cousins with Tricia Houseman's ma? Because the other thing I heard at Home Cookin' this morning was about the little scuffle that Tricia and your woman got into on Saturday. Think there's any connection there?"

Fuck. I didn't even think about that. A feeling of foreboding settles in my gut. "Shit. You're right."

"Maybe you ought to go see her in person and try to get that update. You're pretty persuasive, boss."

Rick comes out of the bathroom and closes the door behind him. Jesus, how long was he in there anyway? I make a mental note to stay far away.

"You ready to finally work today?" I ask Rick.

He laughs and pats his gut. "Sure am now. If I'm gonna spend a couple hours under the car replacing all the gas lines and shit, I figured I better make sure I'm not gonna be getting off that creeper every five minutes. My old lady made chili last night, and that shit is lethal."

I shove the creeper toward him with my foot and it rolls until it stops a few inches away. "Get to it, man. I'm not paying you to spend a half hour taking a shit."

"Got it, boss."

"All right, you two, get to work. I'll go track down Mrs. Borst about the interior. We need to see progress here today."

They both salute me, and I head for the door.

I'm about to climb in my truck when I see a crowd gathering in front of the pharmacy across the street.

"What the hell?"

Figuring I can spare five extra minutes to see what's going on, I shut my door and head over.

What seems like the entire crew of retired folks who normally spend a few hours drinking coffee at Home Cookin' every morning gathers outside. They surround a cameraman as he records a brunette talking about Gold Haven and the recent meth epidemic.

"Can this small town recover? Or are pharmacies like this one going to continue to be targeted for the purchase of supplies to make illegal drugs?" She stops, and the cameraman lowers the camera. "Thanks, Adam. I think that's good."

"Do you wanna interview any of us? We got lots to say," Rita Daws, a former preschool teacher at the Methodist church, asks.

"I'd love to make a list of your names and contact

information so I can follow up with all of you if we need more background," the reporter says. She's probably in her late twenties or early thirties.

"I've got time right now," Rita replies. "But tonight's bingo at the VFW, so I can't promise I'll be available."

The reporter's smile tightens, but she keeps it in place. Rita can be a bit pushy, which is ironic considering her former career.

One of the three Gold Haven police cruisers pulls up alongside the pharmacy.

"Y'all should get back to your coffee. There ain't nothin' to see here."

The crowd quiets, and the woman's attention cuts to the car. It's Ron Timmons, Gold Haven's chief of police.

"Police Chief Timmons!" The woman steps toward the cruiser, gesturing to the cameraman. "I'm Memphis Lockwood of the Investigation Network, I'd love to speak with you about what's happening right now in Gold Haven."

I crane my head to the side, interested to see if he'll actually talk to her. He's one of those retired-on-the-job cops who doesn't do jack. Cody would do a lot better in that position, but until Timmons decides to retire, Gold Haven is pretty much stuck with him because of his close ties with Lester Freeman, the mayor.

"I got a busy schedule at the moment, ma'am. But feel free to check with my secretary down at the station to see if she can squeeze you in."

A few people in the crowd laugh at the obvious line of bullshit, and Timmons's face turns a mottled shade of red, worse than it normally is from hitting the bottle on a nightly basis.

"Police Chief Timmons—" she starts, but Timmons has already rolled up his window and is driving through the blinking red light back to the police station.

"Useless piece of shit," someone murmurs in the crowd, and the reporter zooms in on Eamon Kent, the speaker.

"Do you think that the police department is mishandling this investigation rather than trying to figure out why this town has had such a high incidence of meth-house explosions over the last several weeks?"

The camera is rolling, and Eamon is put on the spot. "I don't know that I can say they're mishandling the investigation so much as not doing any investigating at all. Well, that's not entirely true. Cody Reeves is going around town trying to dig up stuff, but that's about it."

I back away from the crowd. The last thing I want is to show up on national news in some way that's going to have Timmons causing trouble for me. It's not like I have anything to add to the story anyway.

When I cross the street, I hop into my truck, and a text comes through my phone.

BANNER NYC: *My box of dicks is on the way! The post office lady told me they wouldn't deliver to Holly's gran's house, so I had to send them general delivery to the post office. Is that normal?*

I need to take the *NYC* out of her contact, because as far as I'm concerned, that's not who she is anymore. I make the change before I reply.

LOGAN: *They stopped delivering out that way a few*

months back after some budget cuts came down. You'll have to stop in and pick them up.

MY WOMAN: Got it. Can I bring you anything for lunch?

Now that's more like it.

LOGAN: I'm running an errand, so I'll grab something while I'm out.

MY WOMAN: Okay, babe. TTYL

When I slide the phone back in my pocket, it's with a big smile on my face.

EIGHTEEN

Logan

I KNOCK ON THE DOOR TO MRS. BORST'S BREEZEWAY where she has her upholstery shop, and wait a few moments before she opens the door. She stares at me through the screen with a hard look on her face.

"You didn't take me not answering your calls as a response?"

Shit. I decide to play dumb.

"I thought you might not have heard the phone ring, ma'am."

"I heard it. I have that caller ID thingy, so I was screening."

Not a good sign. Time to cut to the chase.

"What do I need to do to get this interior and upholstery finished on time, Mrs. Borst? You going to up the price on me after we already made a deal?"

She shakes her head, her steel-gray curls not budging an inch. "Not for all the money in the world am I touching those panels or seats until your little hussy of a girlfriend apologizes to my cousin and second cousin for what she said about my godson being inbred. That wasn't Minnie's fault. She didn't know she and Lyle were related until after she was pregnant."

Fucking hell. "With all due respect, ma'am, that has nothing to do with the job you said you'd finish for me."

She crosses her arms, thimble still on her bony finger. "That's where you're wrong. No apology, no job."

I want to grab the old woman by the shoulders and shake her, but there's no way I'd ever put my hands on a woman in anger. If I didn't believe in that right down to the marrow of my bones, I would have decked Tricia myself for the shit she was spewing at Banner.

"The job for the apology. That's your stipulation?"

"That's right. And since you said you need this stuff pretty danged quick, you don't have a lot of time to waste screwing around."

"I'll take everything I brought you back right now, and we're done."

Her jaw drops open.

There's no way in hell I'm going to ask Banner to apologize to Tricia, especially not with the black eye Banner had to work hard to cover up this morning.

"What?" Mrs. Borst's tone isn't nearly as forceful as it was only moments ago.

"You weren't there, and I'm sure the story you got from Tricia wasn't the whole truth. If it was, you'd realize you're burning a bridge that doesn't need to be burned."

Her brows wing down into a deep vee. "You need me more than I need you, Brantley. Don't forget about that. Who else do you think can upholster your fancy car seats and fix up those interior pieces in this short of time for this price?"

"I guess I'm about to find out, ma'am, because I'll no longer be needing your services. I'll take my property now and pay you for what you did, but we're done."

"Five hundred dollars and you can take them."

"Let me see how much you finished first."

She steps aside, and I walk into the breezeway to see the pieces of the car interior all over the breezeway workshop.

I cut my gaze to her. "You did the panels and one seat? And you want five hundred dollars?"

She shrugs. "I did the dash too. Don't forget that. The rest is for sunk costs."

Keeping my temper in check, I pull out my wallet and peel off the cash. It's a hit to my budget, but the project is too important to risk.

Mrs. Borst tucks the bills away. "Go on and get your crap out of my workshop." She spins on the heel of her house shoes and leaves the breezeway to head inside the house.

I load all the pieces into the back of my truck before covering them with a tarp, all the while cussing her up and down in my head. *So much for being a professional, Mrs. Borst.*

And now I'm out an upholsterer, and I have no fucking clue what I'm going to do.

NINETEEN

Banner

I PULL INTO THE PARKING LOT OF PIGGLY WIGGLY, desperate to refill my fridge with food after Logan cleared it out for me while I was gone so nothing spoiled. I'm not really excited about small-town grocery shopping today, but I refuse to let the chance of running into anyone nasty get between me and food.

I grab a cart from the parking lot and push it through the automatic doors. As soon as I'm inside, I realize I misjudged my timing. I figured late afternoon on a Monday would be dead, but Piggly Wiggly is as busy as I've ever seen it. Apparently, a lot of the people in this town are already out of work at ten after four.

I make my trip quick, pushing around the perimeter and up a few aisles before making my way to the liquor section. Unfortunately, as soon as I turn the corner, I spot one of the ladies who I tangled with right after I got to Gold Haven. At least this time, that bitch Tricia isn't with her. The brunette grabs a bottle of cheap vodka, and I park my cart right in front of hers and reach for the good stuff on the top shelf.

I don't say a single word to her or even make eye contact, but that doesn't stop her from running her mouth as soon as the bottle touches my cart.

"You just have to rub it in, don't you? That you think you're so much better than us. Wasn't this weekend enough for you?"

It doesn't surprise me that the story of what happened at the bowling alley has already made the rounds, and even more, that whatever story is being told makes me look bad.

"You weren't there, so you might want to get your story straight before you decide to talk about it."

"I didn't need to be there to know that you're more trouble than you're worth to Logan Brantley."

That stings, because I've thought that more than once myself. Regardless, there's no way I'm going to let this woman think she hit a sore spot.

"Again, you don't know what you're talking about." For good measure, I grab another bottle of vodka and push my cart around her, but my exit isn't quite as graceful due to the squeaking cart wheels.

From behind me, she keeps talking. "I know that Logan Brantley is working his butt off on some big project, because Jock was talking about it this morning at Home Cookin'. And I also know as soon as Tricia told her mama's cousin what happened, Mrs. Borst decided she isn't going to finish that upholstery job Logan hired her for until you apologize to both Tricia and her mama for what you said about her brother."

The vodka bottles tip over in my cart with a clatter when I freeze in mid-step.

Slowly, I turn around to face her. "Excuse me?"

The brunette gives me the evil eye. "You heard me. You messed with the wrong family, and now Logan's paying the price in a big way."

And he hasn't told me about any of it.

Refusing to give her any more ammunition to gossip about with her friends, I tell her, "There's absolutely nothing that's going to stop Logan from finishing his project, let alone a bunch of small-minded bitches."

"I guess we'll see about that," she says before turning in a huff and tipping over her own bottles in the process.

I head directly to the checkout lanes. My phone is already in my hand when I join the line, and I text Logan.

BANNER: *Did your upholstery lady quit? Because of me and the bowling alley bitch?*

When he doesn't respond right away, my attention drifts from the lady in front of me with a dozen cases of Dr Pepper on the belt to the rack of tabloids.

I grab the one with a familiar face on the front page.

Cavanaugh Westman Cozy with Billionaire's Sister

Sure enough, there's my best friend, Greer, and her man, Cav, sitting side by side at a sidewalk café somewhere.

My phone buzzes in my hand.

MY SEXY MAN: *Don't worry about it. I'll figure it out.*

My thumbs fly across my screen to reply.

BANNER: *So that's a yes?*
MY SEXY MAN: *It's not your issue. I'll handle it.*
BANNER: *It is my fault. What do I need to do to fix it?*

As much as I hate the thought of apologizing to that bitch, if I have to do it to save Logan's project for Boone, which I know is crazy important for him, I will.

MY SEXY MAN: *You're not doing anything to fix it. I fucking forbid it.*

Whoa now.

BANNER: *You forbid it? Really? You're going there?*
MY SEXY MAN: *Bruce, leave it alone.*
BANNER: *We're talking about this tonight.*
MY SEXY MAN: *I'll call you when I finish up.*

That's not an agreement that we're going to talk, but I have a feeling it's all I'm going to get out of him right now.

My mind starts flipping through options. I don't know anyone who upholsters shit, but someone I know has to.

The woman in front of me pushes her cart out of the checkout line.

"Ma'am, are you ready?" the cashier says, clearly waiting for me.

"Sorry." I unload my cart on the conveyer belt and toss the tabloid on it too. Maybe I'll make a scrapbook for Greer and give it to her someday.

As soon as I've paid and the groceries are loaded up in my rental, I give her a call. She answers on the first ring.

"Hey, B, what's happening? You back in Kentucky?"

"Yes, and don't get me started on the bitches in this town. You need to tell Hollywood that small towns aren't like they portray them in the movies."

"You're more than capable of handling them."

"Of course I am, but it's the repercussions on Logan that's the problem."

"What do you mean?"

I fill her in on everything I haven't already told her, including the bowling alley situation, and the upholstery fallout.

"Good God. Only you, Banner. Only you."

"My life might not be as interesting as yours, Ms. Tabloid Queen."

She groans. "Oh no. What did they print now?"

"Nothing bad. Just you and your hot man." An idea strikes me. "By the way, does he know any of those car show guys? Like the ones that do restorations on TV?"

"You're trying to fix the upholstery situation without having to apologize, aren't you?"

I shrug, but she can't see it. "You know I would in a hot second if Logan asked me to, but I don't think he will. Actually, he forbade it."

"Wait, Logan Brantley *forbid you* from doing something, and you're actually going to listen to him?"

"Normally I only take orders while I'm naked or cock is involved. I might make an exception for this one, but only if I can't find a way to fix it."

Silence follows.

"Greer? Are you still there?"

"Sorry, I'm trying to wrap my head around what you

just said. I never knew you liked it when guys told you what to do in bed. I feel like I don't even know you right now."

"Shut up," I say, feeling my cheeks heat.

"Logan really is different, isn't he?"

I take a deep breath and tell her something I've never told her before. "I'm in love with him."

Greer squeals into the phone. "I knew it! I freaking knew it! I love this so much for you."

"Calm down, *chica*. You're acting like I just cured cancer. It's just a guy."

"But it's not. It's *the* guy. The one who changes everything. You found yours, and that makes me so happy for you."

"Don't get too happy because if I screwed up the most important project he's ever had, things might not be awesome for long."

"Stop it. It's going to be fine. I'll ask Cav. He knows a ton of people, and if he doesn't know someone, he knows someone who knows them. Let me go work this Hollywood connection stuff, and we'll get it figured out."

"I swore I wasn't going to come to you to clean up my messes anymore, G." My tone is quiet, and Greer answers the same way.

"That's what friends are for, babe. Love you."

"Love you."

We hang up, and the knots that formed in my stomach in the liquor aisle loosen a degree.

I'm going to fix this. I will not let Logan's business suffer because of something I did.

TWENTY

Logan

A S I PULL INTO THE GRAVEL DRIVE OF HOLLY'S gran's house, which I still can't think of as Banner's for some reason, the front room is lit up enough that I can see her silhouette through the lace curtains in the front window.

Oh sweet Jesus, it looks like she's standing in front of the stove.

Memories of what happened last time I showed up here to find her cooking rush through my head, including the way that night ended. With me buried balls deep inside her.

I'm out of the truck within moments and striding toward the front door. It's unlocked, so I let myself in. Instead of the scent of something burning, it smells amazing. Browned meat, garlic, and some kind of Italian spice.

Banner spins around at the sound of the door opening. "You're early. I'm not quite done." There's a small, almost hesitant smile on her face.

"Whatcha doin', Bruce?"

"What does it look like, Logan?"

"You're cooking."

She nods slowly. "Got it in one."

I tilt my head to the side, trying to figure out what I'm missing, and Banner picks up on my confusion.

"I, uh . . . took some lessons when I was back in New York."

Surprise filters through me, along with admiration. "Why?"

"Because I figured it was time I learn to feed myself so you don't have to do it all the time."

"You know I don't mind." I say the words, but a warmth pools in the vicinity of my heart. *She learned to cook for me.*

"I wanted to." Banner glances at the bubbling skillet behind her. "I can't promise the results are going to be terribly impressive. It's just spaghetti and meatballs. But I did make the meatballs from scratch."

"It smells fucking amazing, and I'm sure it'll taste the same way. I'm really impressed, babe."

Her eyes widen. "Don't jinx it. I haven't started a single fire or burned anything, so just hold off for a minute." A timer dings on the counter, and she spins around. "That's the pasta."

I step toward her. "Let me drain it for you."

"I wanted to have it all ready as a surprise."

I meet her gaze. "You already did. Besides, we're a team. Let me help."

Banner's smile grows bigger as she steps aside to let me grab the pasta pot off the stove. The colander is already on the kitchen counter, so I make quick work of the process while Banner pulls the garlic bread out of the oven and sets it on the table, followed by the meatballs and sauce. It's a simple meal, but it means a hell of a lot to me that she went to the trouble to learn to make it.

This woman, the one I thought I wouldn't have a damned thing in common with, has proven she fits into my life better than I could have imagined.

We both sit down, a beer in front of my plate and a glass of red wine in front of Banner's.

"I might've already had one or two glasses, but I actually think it helped me chill out and not screw everything up."

She holds her breath while I take my first bite. I chew and give the verdict as soon as I swallow.

"It's amazing."

The pride on her face is obvious as she tries it for herself. "Damn, I did a good job. I think it even tastes delicious."

"Told you."

We both dig in, and Banner waits until I push my plate away after seconds to bring up the subject I figured would come sooner. "Are you going to tell me more about what happened with your upholstery lady?"

"It's my problem to work out, and I will."

"But I caused it."

I shake my head as I finish off my beer. "Tricia caused it, not you. You didn't throw the first punch."

"You know what I mean. I should've kept my mouth shut. How was I supposed to know she had an inbred brother? I thought I was making a ridiculous generalized insult. I can't get over how insane it is that she actually has one."

I lower my beer to the table with a laugh. "They're pretty touchy about it. The story goes that her mama didn't know his daddy was her uncle, but there are plenty of people in this town that dispute it. The story will never die, I swear."

"And I thought New York was crazy."

"It's got nothing on a small town, but let's talk about something else. I've been beating this to death today, and I could really use a distraction."

"I think I can handle that." Banner stands and turns to open the fridge, which is right behind her chair in the small kitchen. "How about some dessert?"

She pulls out a can of whipped cream and a bottle of chocolate syrup.

"And by dessert, I mean me."

TWENTY-ONE

Banner

THESE SHEETS MAY NEVER BE THE SAME, BUT I couldn't care less when Logan's head is between my legs and my back arches as I come for the second time.

"Oh. My. God."

Logan rises up off his knees and lifts my sticky body into the air. "I'm fucking you in the shower."

"Okay." The word comes out on a breath. "But you might have to hold me up. I'm not sure my legs are going to work."

"All you gotta do is keep them wrapped around my waist."

He carries me into the small bathroom and lowers me to my feet, only to strip off his remaining clothes and flip on the water before lifting me up again.

"I'm gonna slide you down on my cock and fuck the hell out of you against the wall."

"How do you feel about the neighbors hearing me scream your name?"

"Fucking phenomenal."

Logan steps up and over the side of the tub and proceeds to do exactly what he promised. He presses me against the tile wall, and inch by inch, he fills me. I have to move my grip from his flexed arms to around his shoulders to steady myself as he pulls back and thrusts inside. My already sensitized clit sings with the friction of his body, and my orgasm builds. Over and over, he fucks into me without slowing or losing his rhythm. My head drops back against the tile as he powers inside. I shift my grip, holding on for dear life as he forces me over the edge.

"Logan!"

His groan fills the shower moments later as he stills, his cock pulsing with his release.

Jesus Christ.

My head lolls to the side as I regain my footing, and he pulls me into his chest. We turn one step at a time until the hot water beats down on my back.

"I love you, baby."

I lift my head to meet his hazy gaze. "Love you right back."

He presses a kiss to my forehead and we stand under the hot spray, saying nothing until it runs cold.

Hours later, my phone buzzes on the nightstand, but Logan is dead to the world in bed next to me. I reach for the phone and read the text from Greer.

BEST BITCH: I found someone who knows someone. I'll be in touch when I have more.

I translate her cryptic message to mean that there's still hope for me to fix what I inadvertently screwed up for Logan.

Banner: Thank you! Love you!
Best Bitch: Love you too. xo

I roll back into Logan's arms, finally able to sleep.

TWENTY-TWO

Logan

O
N SATURDAY, THE ENTIRE TOWN CAME OUT TO celebrate Founder's Day and take part in the parade down Main Street despite the cool temperatures. Same as every year, I volunteered my truck to pull one of the high school floats, but this year Banner is sitting shotgun beside me, her hands wrapped around a thermos of spiked coffee.

We made good progress this week on the Olds 442, but after calling the seven upholsterers within a two-hundred-mile radius, I still have no one to replace Mrs. Borst, regardless of how much money I offer them. No one is willing to take on such a complex project with less than a week to turn it around, and without the custom interior, I'm totally fucked.

I haven't accepted defeat yet, bound and determined that there's no way in hell I'm going to ask Banner to apologize. Despite all its good points, sometimes I really hate living in a small town.

"This is so surreal," Banner says as she gawks out the

passenger window. "I swear, no one must be home right now because every single person in this town is here."

We're almost to the Four Corners, where there's a beer tent and a barbecue competition happening.

"There isn't a lot that happens in Gold Haven except a few festivals, and when there's a beer tent, you can pretty much guarantee everyone is gonna come out and celebrate. Shit, I remember when Holly brought her husband here for WinterFest. If you think you and I get some looks, it's nothing compared to what they got."

Banner's head whips around from the window to face me, her eyebrow raised. "I bet we could give them a run for their money if we tried tonight."

"Easy now. We'll get plenty of attention without even trying. You do remember the bowling alley . . ."

The amusement fades from Banner's expression. "Okay, fine. I'll be on my best behavior. I'm not saying I wasn't then, but I refuse to leave tonight needing another bag of tater tots."

Her shiner is barely visible today, at least not with makeup hiding the fading colors.

"I think that's a good plan, babe. I'll buy you a beer, feed you some barbecue, and we can people watch before I take you home and keep you up most of the night."

"Deal."

She winks as we slow to wait for the parade traffic to turn left and park in various lots up the next block. We take another left and pull into the alley behind my shop to unhook the float. One of the kids' dads will be by to tow it away later.

Outside Cut a Bitch, Julianne has a big table, and all

her stylists are handing out flyers and little pink bags to the people walking by.

After we park, I help Banner out of the cab, and all the high school kids hop off the float and head toward the food. I wrap an arm around my woman and steer her in the same direction.

Julianne waves when she sees us. "Nice cover-up job!"

Banner salutes her, but the makeup doesn't hide the pink her cheeks are taking on. "Jesus Christ, it's been a week already. How long do you think it'll take before people forget about that?"

I look down at her. "Do you want the truth or do you want me to lie?"

Her brows draw together. "I'm not sure."

I try to keep the smile off my face. "I'm sure they'll forget by next weekend."

She pulls away, or at least attempts it, but I'm not letting her go anywhere. "You're lying. No one is ever going to forget, are they?"

"Probably not, but look at it this way. It's unlikely anyone else is going to try to take you on. You held your own."

Banner rolls her eyes. "I got my ass kicked. I probably need a rematch so I can redeem myself."

"Whoa, cage fighter. I think once was enough."

"I don't care if her brother's dad is really her new used-to-be-sister. Or whatever. If she comes at me again—"

I cup the side of Banner's face and press my thumb to her lips, trying not to laugh. "Now *that* you don't have to worry about. And she won't."

Banner closes her eyes for a beat before meeting mine. "Moving on."

"Good. How do you feel about barbeque?"

She presses a hand to her stomach. "Feed me. I need all the food."

"That I can do."

We make our way through the line, filling our tray with barbeque, baked potatoes, corn, and pie. Once our plates are full, we find seats across from each other at the end of one of the picnic tables under the tents covering Main Street.

"I'm going to grab some beer. You want one?"

Banner taps the bottle of water she picked up in line. "I'm good. I forgot for a hot second that I don't actually like beer. Besides, this way I can drive if you need me to."

"Fair enough." I give her a nod before heading up to the crew serving beer in the next tent. The line moves quickly, which isn't surprising because Nicole is working.

"Hey, Logan, what'll you have?"

"Whatever's good tonight."

She turns around and grabs two plastic cups already filled with a light-colored beer.

"This is my favorite of what we've got on tap." She pauses. "Banner okay after the other night? That shit was pretty epic."

I shove my hand in my back pocket to pull out my wallet. "She's fine." I hand the money over and am about to say more when Cody steps up to the side of the bar.

"Can I get you something, Officer?" Nicole asks him.

"I need you to come with me, Nicole. I've got a few questions for you."

I freeze, my hands wrapped around the cups as I watch the exchange, everything Emmy said about Nicole coming back to me. *There's no way . . .*

Nicole gestures to the taps and the line behind me. "Can't it wait? I'm working."

"You're a harder woman to track down than I would've thought. I've been out to your place three times, and I seem to keep missing you." The way Cody says it makes it sound like he thinks she's dodging him on purpose.

"I'm sorry your timing is shit, but I can't leave now."

The serious expression on Cody's face stays put. "Right now I'm asking. Don't make me tell you."

Nicole blinks. "Are you threatening to arrest me?"

"I'm telling you that I have questions to ask you in connection with an ongoing investigation, and I'm done chasing you around this town trying to get answers."

"Questions about what?"

"You don't want me to go into it here."

"We got a problem here?" Jordan Birch, the beer distributor in town and the man responsible for the beer tents, comes up behind Nicole. "Because I got beer to sell, and this line ain't getting any shorter."

"You need to find someone to take over the rest of Nicole's shift. She's coming with me."

Jordan's gaze cuts to Nicole and back to Cody. "What the hell is going on?"

"Fine. I'll go. But only because I don't want to give the assholes in this town more to talk about, which is exactly what's going to happen if you drag me out of here." Her tone is ripe with frustration, and maybe a little fear. She gives Cody a hard look. "Do I need to call a lawyer?"

The cop shrugs. "If you feel like you need one. That's up to you."

She straightens her shoulders. "I've got nothing to hide, but I know how this goes. You're going to automatically assume I did something wrong if I call one. So, fuck it, I'll follow you to the station and you can ask your questions. This is bullshit, for the record."

Nicole knocks a stack of plastic cups off the temporary bar and strides off. Cody is on her heels, and the fact that he's not about to let her out of his sight makes me wonder exactly what he's got on her.

What the hell is this town coming to?

TWENTY-THREE

Banner

APPARENTLY ALL I HAD TO DO IF I WANTED PEOPLE to stop talking about my epic bowling alley catfight was wait for the next big piece of gossip to hit Gold Haven. I didn't have to wait long.

"Did you hear that Cody Reeves just arrested Nicole Hiram?"

"What?"

The conversation starts at the picnic table backed up to the one I'm sitting at before Logan returns with his beer. I search the crowd for him and see him moving my way. As soon as he sits down, I whisper, "I just heard that Nicole—"

His expression turns dark. "Jesus, it just happened. People are fucking fast when it comes to gossip."

"So it's true." My whisper gets a little louder.

Logan shakes his head. "He just asked her to come in to answer some questions. That's all."

The buzz of conversation behind us grows louder, and Logan's gaze lifts over my shoulder.

"So she's the one responsible for all those houses exploding?

Just to buy that bowling alley? Shameful what people will do for money these days."

"Isn't it, though? I always knew there was something off about that girl."

Logan's fisted hands clench tighter on the table, his knuckles turning white. He can't protect her from this gossip, and I know it must be pissing him off. The last thing he needs is to blow up and have people talking about him, though.

"Do you want to take this home?" I ask. Our dinners are already in to-go containers, so transport is no issue.

Logan grabs a beer and chugs it before nodding.

"I'll drive," I say as he slams the second one back. I just want to get us out of here.

We're out of the tent and walking toward his truck minutes later.

"I don't fucking believe it," Logan says, his voice low and frustrated. "There's no way Nicole would get mixed up in that stuff. She's not built like that. Why the fuck would she bust her ass like she has been, and then all of a sudden decide to take the easy way out?"

He opens the driver's side door for me and helps me into the cab of the truck. I have approximately thirty seconds to work out some kind of response to his question before he climbs in.

"I'm not saying she did, but maybe . . . sometimes people who are busting their asses all the time but can't seem to catch a break get desperate, and when an easier solution comes along, they might be in a position where it doesn't sound like the worst idea in the world."

Logan slams a fist against the dash. "That's not her.

I've known her forever, and I refuse to fucking believe she could do something like that."

I fire up the truck and look at him, no longer able to hold back the question that's been on my mind ever since I heard the first whisper of gossip tonight. "Why was she forty miles away, late at night, getting shut down when she tried to buy something at the pharmacy?"

He turns and gives me a hard look. "There's gotta be another explanation. Like why you had pregnancy tests but didn't even think you were pregnant."

"Touché." I shift the truck into drive. "Where are we headed? Your house or mine?"

"I'm not up for sleeping in that tiny bed of yours tonight."

"Okay." I turn the wheel in the direction of Logan's house.

The silence that normally hangs between us is comfortable and easy, yet tonight it's anything but. I'm practically squirming in the driver's seat because of how awkward it feels, and I don't know what to say to fix it.

"Maybe the fact that they're questioning Nicole is good. They're actually taking the investigation more seriously now, right?"

Logan leans back in his seat, his hands now clenching his thighs. "Because national news picked it up and that reporter chick came to town. Chief Timmons will look incompetent if he doesn't get off his ass and start trying to get to the bottom of it now."

"Which reporter chick?" I turn on the blinker to go left at the next intersection.

"Memphis something from the Investigation Network."

My eyes cut to Logan. "Memphis Lockwood? She's a big freaking deal. I've seen her report on things in New York. Mostly corruption cases and controversial topics."

"Yeah, that one. She's here in town."

Shock ripples through me as I wait for a car to turn before continuing on. If Memphis Lockwood is here, Gold Haven is about to get more attention than when Holly Wix won *Country Dreams* and became a star.

"Let's hope she doesn't hear about Nicole being questioned, because that's the last thing she needs to know."

Logan looks out the window. "Yeah, let's hope."

TWENTY-FOUR

Banner

T HE REST OF THE WEEKEND IS SUBDUED, AND although the gossips are still talking about Nicole, she's kept a low profile. Part of me wants to seek her out, but I don't know what good it would do. When Logan isn't spending all hours at the shop working on Boone's car, he's quiet, so I know the situation is eating at him.

Early Monday morning, I get a text from Greer about the car upholstery.

BEST BITCH: *What would you say if I told you Cav called in a favor, and Elliott Crisp from the show Tricked Out has someone in Nashville who can do the seats on Boone's car?*

I have no idea what *Tricked Out* is, so I do a quick Google search. Apparently it's a show on a major cable network where they take junkyard wrecks and turn them into show cars in a ridiculously short amount of time. *Holy shit. This might actually work.*

BANNER: No fucking way! Are you serious?

BEST BITCH: Logan just has to get all the seats and the design to him in Nashville before tomorrow morning and they'll take it from there.

BANNER: They can be ready in a few days? How much will it cost?

BEST BITCH: What do you care? You're a baller who inherited 30 mil.

She's right, I don't care. But Logan will.

BANNER: OMFG, you're amazing! You just saved my ass from having to apologize to those bitches. Can you send me the contact info?

Greer sends it through, along with an *xo*.

I call immediately and talk to the guy. The price is steep, but he and I make a deal that I'll cover the hefty rush fee, and Logan will get a bill for the rest. As soon as I have his word that he can make this happen and Logan will never know about the total price we agreed on, I run out to my rental car and jump in, not caring that I only have eyeliner on one eye and zero mascara.

Shit, I really do love him if I'm willing to leave the house like this.

When I pull into the parking lot of Logan's shop, I can barely contain my excitement. As per usual, the music is pounding, and all three men are working on the Olds 442 that's almost completely finished but for the paint job and the interior.

"Logan!"

Logan steps away from the car when he sees me and turns down the music. "Everything okay, Bruce?"

I nod my head. "Everything is so much better than okay. I found someone who can do your upholstery, and I don't have to apologize to Tricia."

"What are you talking about?"

"You just have to get the seats to Nashville ASAP, and this guy who does this show about tricking out cars has someone who can do the work there. His name is Elliott something." My explanation comes out in a big babble, and Logan's eyebrows knit together as he processes it.

"Elliott Crisp? From *Tricked Out*? Are you fucking serious?"

I nod again, probably a little too vigorously. "Yeah, I asked Greer, and she said she owes you, so her man called in a favor, and this Elliott guy's friend can do it."

Logan tilts back his head and stares at the ceiling for a moment, making me wonder if I misjudged how helpful I'm being. When he meets my gaze with his blue eyes shining, my question is answered.

"You're a goddamned lifesaver, babe. I wonder how much it's gonna cost me."

"It's a favor, so regular price is all you have to pay."

"Thank fuck. Where do I need to take them?"

I release a sigh of relief. "I'll text you the address."

He looks over at his employees. "Yo, Jock. Rick. You can hold down the fort, right? I gotta get the seats to Nashville right the fuck now to save our asses."

The one with Jock embroidered on the patch on his shirt replies. "Sure thing, man. Not much more to do before we deliver this to the paint shop. We'll finish it all up."

I send the address to Logan while he changes out of his coveralls and pulls a long-sleeved shirt over the T-shirt he's wearing.

"You coming with me, babe?"

When I hesitate, Logan's eyes widen. "Shit, your . . . stuff is being delivered today, isn't it?" And by stuff, he means my box of dicks, but he chooses his words carefully, no doubt because of our audience.

"Yeah, but—"

Logan shakes his head. "No buts. You stay here and wait for it. That's way more important for you." He pulls me far enough away from where Jock and Rick are standing so they don't overhear what he says next. "But tonight I want to come home and find you in my bed, playing with one of your toys. I'm gonna sit and watch you get yourself off before I make you come to compare."

And just like that, my panties are a lost cause. "Oh yeah?"

"Fuck yeah."

"Deal."

Logan leans in and gives me a quick, hard kiss. "I'm gonna be hard all fucking day while I'm driving."

Several hours later, I get an e-mail from the shipping company that my boxes have been delivered via general delivery to the Gold Haven post office. Given that it's almost four o'clock, I rush out of the house for the second time this afternoon, although this time I've got all my eye makeup on. *Winning.*

There are no spots in front of the post office, so I park

in front of Cut a Bitch and hop out. Julianne bangs on the window to get my attention.

I wave but keep walking, racing the clock to get my stuff before closing time. When she bangs again in what I assume is a response, I'm already pushing open the door to the post office.

The line is three people deep, and I impatiently wait my turn. Finally, I reach the counter.

"I'm here to pick up two packages." I turn my phone around to show her the delivery notification.

The woman takes my phone and props it up against her monitor. She taps the tracking numbers into the computer using the hunt-and-peck method, testing my patience further.

Her expression twists with what I assume is confusion, but she types it in again before looking up at me. "I'm sorry, but these have already been picked up."

"Excuse me?" My voice rises, and all the other conversations in the tiny post office halt.

She clears her throat. "Yes, ma'am. It says here that someone already picked these up today."

"That's impossible. They're my packages. No one else would be here to pick them up."

She scans down the page, shaking her head. "Maybe there was some kind of mistake?"

"Obviously there was some sort of mistake if you gave them to someone who wasn't me." My temper flares to peak levels as my patience hits rock bottom. "Who did you give them to? Where are they?"

The man at the next station over comes to stand behind the woman helping me. "Which packages are y'all going on about?"

The woman points to the computer screen. "These two."

"Emmy Harris was in here earlier picking up a dozen boxes for Home Cookin'. I wonder if there was some sort of mix-up when I carted them over there for her."

At the name Emmy Harris, I want to scream. I swear, that woman keeps popping up everywhere, and each time, she's a bigger pain in my ass.

The man goes back to his computer terminal. "Hmm. I might've made a mistake." He looks at me. "I'm sorry, ma'am. I think I might've been so caught up in loading her stack that I grabbed a couple extras and tossed them on."

My head feels like it's about to explode. "Then you can go get them back for me, right?" Home Cookin' is just across the street, so it's not like it'll be hard for him.

"Sorry, I can't leave until after I close up and count down all the drawers. If you want them now, you can go check with her. Ms. Harris is just as sweet as can be, so I'm sure she'll have no issue handing them right over."

A strangled sound escapes from my throat. "Are you serious? You're not going to bother to fix your mistake? You're going to make me do it?"

He shrugs like it's no big deal. "Everyone screws up occasionally. It's not like you can't get them back from her. Now, feel free to step out of line so we can help the next customer."

This. Can't. Be. Happening.

But when a woman steps up beside me and starts talking to the postal clerk, it appears this really is happening.

What the hell is wrong with this town?

I stomp out of the post office and find myself back on

the sidewalk, wondering if there's a thing as professionalism that exists anymore.

"Hey ho!"

Apparently not.

Jerking my head to the left, I see Julianne sticking her head out of the salon door and waving.

"I'll be right back," I yell and keep walking.

"But—"

"Later!"

I cross the street and head for the front door of Home Cookin', ready to get my boxes back and get on with my day.

When I push open the door and stride up to the counter, the conversation at the big table full of retired ladies having coffee hushes, but their version of quiet still allows me to hear every single word they say.

"Oh my word, is that her?"

"Yep. She's the one."

A prickle of foreboding creeps up the back of my neck, but I ignore it.

The waitress Darlene stops in front of me with a smirk on her face. "I can guess what you're here for."

"I need to talk to Emmy."

She huffs out a laugh. "I'll just bet you do."

You've got to be kidding me.

When Darlene walks away, I swing around to face the whispers that were coming from behind me. The women look away as I tap my foot and wait.

Finally, Darlene returns from the back, and Emmy is right behind her.

"I think you have two boxes of mine that the post office

gave you by mistake," I tell her, not bothering to waste her time or mine with a greeting.

Emmy leans on the counter, and I can't read her expression. "Just when I think one person can't cause any more scandal in this wholesome small town of ours, I'm proven wrong."

I roll my eyes. "Just give me the boxes, and we can forget this ever happened."

"Oh, I don't think my good friend Tricia is going to forget what she saw in my office just twenty minutes ago. A box full of . . . I can't even say it."

Tricia. Fuck.

"Let me guess. She was so scandalized, she had to go tell the entire town that you accidentally opened a box of dicks not meant for you."

Emmy's sharp inhale tells me I've hit my mark. "Don't you have any shame at all? Or even self-respect? What is Logan going to think of this when he finds out what kind of things you're getting sent here—"

I adopt the sweetest tone I can manage and interrupt her. "Oh, honey, if you think he doesn't know and one hundred percent support the idea, then you're just sad and misguided."

Her mouth drops open.

"Yeah, that's right. In fact, if you'll just give me my stuff, I'll be able to follow through on what he asked me to do tonight, which is be at his house waiting for him, getting myself off."

"I've never—"

"Had a decent orgasm? Just give me a few more weeks, and my company will be able to sell you a product to fix that."

Now it's not just Emmy gasping for air like a fish, because I hear the same noise coming from behind me as well. I turn in a circle, my arms flung wide, and pitch my voice so no one misses what I have to say.

"That's right, ladies. I like dick. Lots of dick. Luckily for me, I'm getting the good dick. But even more luckily for you, I can make sure you get the good dick too. Orgasms for everyone!"

A slow clap starts, and my eyes cut to the door where Julianne stands.

"Oh. My. God. That was fucking priceless."

"You can take your boxes, but we don't need any of your disgraceful things here." Emmy spins and heads for the back.

I make a move to follow her, but pause when another round of slow clapping starts. I turn back to see six of the women in the group of retirees standing.

"Don't listen to her, honey. We want the good dick too," one says.

"I'll take two of everything you've got, if they work. My sister Agnes will want them for sure."

All of a sudden, more women are leaving the table and coming toward me with questions about what I've got in my boxes that can help their boxes.

Julianne joins the crowd, but can't stop laughing.

This day is looking up. Maybe, just maybe, I'm not too scandalous for the women of Gold Haven.

When I leave Home Cookin', Julianne hefts one box,

remarking that two boxes of dicks are too much for any woman to handle, and helps me carry it to my car.

"I honestly don't know where I found my entertainment before you came to town," she says. "Seriously, that was the best speech I've heard anyone give. I think you should run for mayor. You'd win by a landslide because our female population vastly outnumbers the male. Plus, with a slogan like *orgasms for everyone*, you really can't go wrong."

"Stop it. Jesus. Logan is going to be hearing about this before he even gets home, I'm sure."

"Probably, but I can't imagine he's going to have a lot to say because you made sure to tell everyone that you're getting the good dick."

I shift the box to my hip as we reach my rental car to dig the keys out of my pocket and pop the trunk. "True. I did brag about him. Because he does have the best dick. If I weren't so greedy about keeping it all to myself, I'd make a mold of it to base my next product line on. But there's no way in hell I'm sharing his dick with the world, so that won't be happening."

"That's just selfish, but then again, I can't blame you," Julianne says. "Damn, I wish I'd gotten that little speech of yours on video. It was seriously epic." She sets the box in the trunk, and I shove the second one in next to it.

I flip open the top of the one that's open. *Thank you very much, Emmy*. I pull out a beautifully packaged vibrator and hand it to Julianne. "Try it. See how you like it."

Her eyes widen and she claps her hands together like it's Christmas. "Are you serious? I wanted one, but I didn't want to ask. I was about to lose the battle and ask anyway."

"If you tried to leave without one, I would've just

shoved it at you anyway. You can be my spokesperson."

"Fuck yes, I can. If they're as awesome as you say, I want to be an authorized distributor. This would be the best addition to the tools my shop sells since that killer flat iron I brought in last year."

I dig through the box and pull out another package. "Here. Take this one too. Tell me which one you like best."

She hugs both to her chest. "Seriously, you might be the best thing to happen to this town since Logan came back. Don't let Emmy Harris or that bitch Tricia run you out of here. Gold Haven needs you."

With those words, she strolls back toward her hair salon, and through the window, I see her hold up both boxes. A moment later, the four women inside start clapping. Julianne looks back at me through the front window and winks.

Maybe I do belong here.

TWENTY-FIVE

Logan

AFTER WHAT SEEMS LIKE AN ENTIRE DAY ON THE road, I finally pull into my driveway. The fatigue and tension from driving fades as soon as I see Banner's car parked in front of my garage. It's something I could easily get used to.

I hop out of the truck and head inside through the back door, shutting it quietly so as not to give away my presence. My dick is already hard at the thought of what she might be doing in my bed right now. As I walk toward my bedroom, my anticipation rises with each step.

When I reach the doorway, I stop and thank every higher power for putting this woman in my life.

Because, holy fucking Christ, there is nothing I did to deserve this.

Banner is spread out on top of my sheets like some kind of fantasy come to life, wearing nothing but a scrap of red lace that she might call a bra, but I can see her nipples through. Her legs are splayed wide, and there's a toy buried inside her pussy. Her eyes are closed as she throws her head back and lets out a moan.

She doesn't even realize I'm here, and she's already getting off. Naughty girl.

I pull off one boot and let it fall heavy on the floor. Banner's eyes pop open, and she turns her head toward the sound.

"Couldn't wait for me?"

Instead of looking sheepish, she lets a smug smile stretch over her heart-stoppingly beautiful face. "Just getting warmed up. Have I mentioned that I might be a design genius? This thing is really freaking amazing."

I focus on the toy as she slides it in and out, a faint buzzing now audible. "Is that right? You like your fake cock more than you like the real thing?"

She tsk-tsks before pulling it free. "No need to get jealous. I'm sure by now more than half the town is well aware that I'm getting the good dick, and it's not this fake one."

I pause as I lean down to pull off my other boot. "Come again?"

Banner proceeds to tell me what I missed this afternoon at Home Cookin'.

It's official; she's the perfect woman. No one else could possibly make me laugh so much while my dick is this hard.

"Jesus, Bruce. You never cease to amaze me." I slide off my remaining boot and reach for the button of my jeans.

"I think it's time you show me what that thing can do. Can it make you scream like me?"

"I guess we'll see."

I tug my shirt over my head, and shove my jeans and boxer briefs off my hips before kneeling on the bed and trailing a finger down Banner's impressive cleavage. "I don't think I've paid these perfect tits nearly enough attention lately."

She smiles up at me as she drags the toy over her clit. "Then by all means . . . feel free."

Banner pushes the toy into her pussy, and part of it buzzes over her clit while I lean down and suck one nipple through the red lace. When it puckers exactly the way I want, I switch to the other and give it the same attention.

Her eyes are closed, and I take a moment to appreciate every inch of this incredible woman. Her head tilts back on the pillow and her hips buck into the air as she moans my name over and over, each time louder than the last.

It's the sexiest sound I've ever heard.

When she finally comes, my cock is harder than tempered steel, and pre-cum leaks from the tip.

Banner's head falls to the side, and I cover her hand on the toy with mine. "It's my turn to make you scream my name."

Her eyelids flick open. "Bring it."

I slide the toy free of her body, unable to resist lowering my head to taste how fucking sweet she is. Within minutes, she's writhing against my face, ready to go off again.

"How can you do this to me?"

I pull back and notch my cock into her entrance. "Because you were fucking made for me."

And with that declaration, I drive home, the word *mine* on my lips.

TWENTY-SIX

Banner

BANNER: *Can you die from too many orgasms?*

BEST BITCH: *Now you're just bragging.*

BANNER: *Maybe a little.*

BEST BITCH: *You're lucky I love you, AND that I'm having all the amazing orgasms of my own that I can handle.*

BANNER: *Love you too, G. Miss you.*

BEST BITCH: *Miss you too. xo*

I lay my phone on the side table and roll over in bed. I'm not sure I'm capable of having another orgasm for at least twenty-four hours. Logan kept me up most of the night, fucking me over and over. At first, I thought it was a man-pride thing, wanting to prove that my vibrator couldn't compete with him, but when he pushed into my ass and grabbed the vibrator to play with my pussy, I changed my mind. He was trying to kill me with pleasure.

My entire body is so languid, I'm not sure I ever want to get out of this bed. The shower shuts off, and Logan walks out of the bathroom a few minutes later, wearing nothing but a towel.

I decide I was actually waiting in bed for this very sight. My lady parts, which got the most intense workout of their life last night and should be in hibernation, tingle with appreciation.

A drop of water slides between his pecs and down his tight, flat stomach. Suddenly, the will to move springs into my limbs, if only to chase that droplet with my tongue.

"It's not fair that you can look that good after stepping out of the shower. I should have a CLOSED FOR BUSINESS sign over my vagina after last night, but now I want to climb you."

Logan's grin doesn't help smother my urge.

"My dick should be broken from how many times we went at it last night, but one look at you all curled up in my bed will always get me hard again, Bruce. You're fucking beautiful, no makeup, wild hair, and that sexy hunger in your eyes."

His words fill my chest with warmth. "Damn, you sure know how to make a girl feel pretty in the morning."

Logan shakes his head. "Not pretty. Beautiful."

"Charmer."

"Only for you."

I sit up, holding the covers to my chest. "So, what's next on your agenda?"

"Besides wishing I could stay in bed all day with you?"

He and I both know with his deadline coming up at the end of the week and my new sample products here, that's not an option. Sometimes being a responsible adult sucks, but I guess the tradeoffs make it worth it. Most of the time.

"I gotta get the Olds over to the paint shop, which is

going to be a bitch without any interior, and hope like hell they can execute the design I drew for them."

I'm hoping they can too because I know how much Logan has riding on this car. "It'll be perfect. I have faith."

"What about you?"

"A call with the factory since I've tried out the final samples and know they work great." I shoot him a wink. "Another call with my marketing firm to finalize a launch date once I have expected production dates from the factory. Basically, a shit load of work that I can't wait to tackle."

Maybe adulting doesn't suck so bad after all. There's something totally different about working for yourself instead of working for someone else that makes busting your ass not suck.

"Good for you, babe. We both have a full plate right now."

I don't mention that I have to talk to my financial adviser and lawyers too because there are more things I have to sign to complete the transfer of all of Myrna's property to me. Logan and I haven't really discussed my inheritance again, and I haven't been in a hurry to bring it up. I don't want to make him uncomfortable.

When I was semi-broke and needing to live in Holly's gran's house because I got evicted from my apartment, he didn't have an issue with me. Although, I didn't tell him my being broke was a temporary thing regardless because of my trust fund, but then again, he didn't need to know that either. I'm still exactly who I am. Having a safety net that's not capped on an annual basis doesn't change a whole lot, except now I can invest more in my business.

When Logan drops his towel in front of the dresser,

all thoughts evaporate from my brain except *holy shit, that man is perfection.*

I scoot to the edge of the bed. "If you want to bring that beautiful dick over here, I think I can make this morning a whole lot better for both of us."

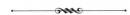

After Logan leaves the house a *very* happy man, I shower and toss my stuff in my bag before heading out to my car to go home. Never in my life have I considered moving in with a guy, but this going-back-and-forth stuff is getting old. We've said the "I love yous," and I know Logan would flip his shit if I suddenly planned to leave Gold Haven, but we haven't exactly gotten to the discussion of where we go from this point.

It's completely foreign territory to me. Relationships weren't exactly on the Banner Regent to-do list, so I have no actual clue what comes next. I have a feeling moving in together is the next logical step, but I'm not going to bring it up. What if he doesn't want me in his space all the time?

I can picture me saying something about it and then awkward silence coming from Logan.

Nope. Definitely not going there.

One thing I've always done is rush headlong into things without stopping to consider the consequences, but this I don't want to rush and screw up.

Or maybe I'm just being a wimp about it because I can't face the idea that maybe Logan would be happy to keep things exactly the way they are.

I guess I'll just have to wait and see.

In the meantime, I'm going to enjoy the now.

TWENTY-SEVEN

Logan

"**B**OSS, YOU GOT A VISITOR." JOCK'S VOICE echoes across the garage to the back corner where my office is hidden.

Now that I'm waiting on the paint shop and the upholsterer to do their parts in making Boone's 442 kick ass, I'm playing catch-up on some of the other things I let slide around the shop. Namely, all the shit piled on my desk. There's a landslide of paper, and even though I've been sorting for ten minutes, you can't tell I've touched a thing. Jock's interruption is welcome at this point.

I step out of the office and make my way across the shop. Rick is finishing up a brake job for one of the ladies who works at the pharmacy, so at least there's some money coming in today. Jock winks at me as he steps out of the doorway between the garage and the customer waiting area.

What the hell?

I step inside to find a brunette in a black trench coat waiting with a notepad tucked under her arm. The reporter.

I recognize her from the crowd the other day.

"I'll leave you two alone," Jock says. "It was nice to meet you, Ms. Lockwood."

She nods at him and then extends a hand to me. "Hi, Mr. Brantley. I'm Memphis Lockwood of the Investigation Network. Thank you for making time to speak with me. I really appreciate it."

"I haven't agreed to speak with you yet."

Her shoulders stiffen only the slightest at my blunt statement, but it doesn't put her off.

"Don't write me off just yet, Mr. Brantley. I'm not here to cause trouble. I received an anonymous tip a few weeks back that there was something of an epidemic happening in Gold Haven, and the local police aren't doing much about it. The newsroom didn't become interested until I did some digging and found the connection to Holly Wix. Just like that, I had a story I wanted to tell, and the network was happy about the prospect for ratings."

Out of everything she says, one thing stands out. *An anonymous tip? From who?*

She's waiting for a response, so I go with the most basic one. "My name's Logan or Brantley, but not Mr. Brantley."

"Okay, Logan. Is there anything you can tell me about what's going on?"

"I don't know any more than what I've heard on the radio, Ms. Lockwood."

"You can call me Memphis, and I'm not sure I believe that completely. It seems like you've got a central location, and most of the townspeople stop in here at one point or another. I'm sure you've heard your share of gossip."

I cross my arms over my chest. "We get plenty of traffic,

but I don't have any answers for you."

"And yet the police have interviewed you more than once in connection to the case."

"Where did you hear that?"

She nods toward the shop. "Your employee was very helpful. I understand you used to be related to a man who had a near-fatal overdose, and actually helped save his life. And what's more, the body of one of your former employees was found in a meth-house fire. Is that correct?"

Jock needs to learn to keep his goddamned mouth shut.

"That's all true, but there's nothing more I can tell you than what I told the cops. I hadn't seen Jeff since the last time he came around wanting money, and Roy Planter hadn't worked here in months."

"But still, the connections—"

"You're in a small town, Ms. Lockwood. You don't have to look hard to find connections between most people. This is the kind of place where the majority of people stay put rather than leave."

"So you wouldn't say that your connection to Nicole Hiram is worthy of discussing either, even though Officer Reeves questioned her Saturday night? I understand she used to work here as well on occasion, and you've been friends for a long time."

I give the reporter a hard look. "What is it you want from me, ma'am? You want me to speculate on who I think is responsible? Because I don't have a clue. If I did, maybe Cody could go out and arrest him, because we all know Timmons isn't doing jack shit."

"The lack of concern from the police chief about my anonymous tip is what really got me interested. There's nothing I like less than people with power not using it the way they're supposed to."

"Then we agree on that. There's nothing else I can tell you that you probably haven't heard from someone else."

"But I want to hear it from you, Mr. Brantley. You know the players. You have a stake in this town getting back to normal."

"If I knew who had a hand in all this, you better believe I would do something about it. You don't have to ask too many people to find out that Jeff wasn't smart enough to mastermind his way out of a paper bag, let alone some kind of drug operation. Or that Roy Planter was an alcoholic who needed money, and his morals weren't the best, especially when he was desperate."

"And what about Nicole Hiram?"

"She's one of the hardest-working people I know, and if you want me to believe for a minute that she's got something to do with this, you're wasting your breath."

The reporter furiously scrawls notes on her pad, and looks up at me when she stops. "But what about the bowling alley? I've been told she's trying to raise money to buy it." She looks down at her pad. "Pints and Pins. Isn't that enough motive in itself?"

Again, the memory of Nicole trying and failing to buy something at the pharmacy the night Banner and I were there for lube comes back to me.

Still, I'm firm when I reply. "No. It's not. Because if she was looking for an easy way out, she would've taken it long before now. I've got a lot of work to do today, ma'am, and I really need to get back to it."

She flips her notepad shut and meets my gaze.

"Mr. Brantley. Logan. This isn't a witch hunt being sensationalized for national TV."

"Then why the hell are you here?"

"Because I'm from a small town in the Midwest that's not much different from Gold Haven, and if this were happening in my town, I'd want to know who was behind it. A huge cross-section of our viewing public can relate to the issues this town is facing. Meth is a nationwide epidemic, especially in our rural areas. I'm hoping that if people can see Gold Haven succeed at getting back to normal, it'll give my viewers hope as well."

Her impassioned speech finally gets through to me, but that doesn't mean I'm going to offer up any idle speculation without facts.

"I appreciate what you're trying to do, Ms. Lockwood. But you're better off talking to the cops and firemen who've been dealing with the crime scenes directly. They're the ones who are going to be able to give you the most information. I've got nothing else I can tell you."

"So that's a no to being interviewed on camera?" she asks, a smile twitching her lips because she already knows what I'm going to say.

"No, thank you. But go look up Granger Ryan down at the fire station. He might actually have something useful for you."

She tucks her notepad under her arm and shoves her pen in her pocket. "Already tried. He declined to comment."

"Then I guess you're shit out of luck for the moment."

She flashes a smile. "You don't know much about reporters, do you, Mr. Brantley? We're a tenacious breed. I didn't get to where I am by letting people stonewall me. I'm going to figure this out. Maybe I'll stop by and chat with Mr. Ryan and Officer Reeves again. They don't understand how determined I am, but they will."

"Good luck to you, ma'am."

Memphis Lockwood nods and turns for the door.

God help Granger and Cody.

I have a feeling Memphis Lockwood is a pit bull when she locks onto something.

TWENTY-EIGHT

Logan

On Wednesday, I'm back on the road to Nashville to pick up the seats. I have to get them back to my shop and in the car after the paint's done before I turn around and drive my truck and trailer back down this same road to deliver the Olds 442 to Boone Thrasher.

The miles don't matter, though, only the final product does. With my eyes fixed on the road, I let my mind wander a little in the quiet of the truck about how much this one job could change things for me.

Getting my shop on the map is all it takes. High-end restorations carry a hefty enough price tag that I might be able to expand and hire a few more guys.

There's a kid at the trade school one town over who called yesterday morning to see if I'd consider taking him on part time, and it sucked to say that I couldn't just yet, but to give me a few months and check back.

For me, owning a business isn't just about making money and being respectable, it's about how I can use my business to help the people in the community too. I need to hire someone to deal with clients and paperwork, but I've been holding off until I know I won't have to let someone go as quick as I hire them. I also need a few more techs to deal with a heavier volume of cars and to shorten our turn-around time. Hell, I'd even love to have my own paint shop someday so I could keep that piece of the work in-house and have more control over it.

My dreams are big, but right now, I gotta focus on what's possible.

Then there's Banner.

The woman inherits $30 million and barely even mentions it beyond calls with a lawyer and a financial adviser here and there. Maybe that's the difference between people who've always had money and people who haven't. Sure, her parents cut her off when she was in college, but maybe it's something that's ingrained in you. I've never had it, so I can't say.

I should be relieved that Banner's attitude hasn't changed since she got that money. I mean, shit, if anyone in Gold Haven won the lottery tomorrow, which is essentially what she did, they'd be driving a brand-new car and flashing it all over town. Banner's still driving the rental car Holly and Creighton leased for her.

Speaking of which, my woman needs better wheels than a Toyota Camry, but it's not something she's ever complained about.

Banner is a surprise on every level. The way she's adapted to living here is nothing short of a miracle. There's no Starbucks on every corner, and no sushi unless you eat the fish raw you caught yourself, which I wouldn't recommend.

Other than a comment here and there about something she misses in New York, Banner seems to be settling in well.

It pisses me off that some of the women in this town have given her hell, but after the bowling alley incident with Tricia and the box of dicks with Emmy, I'm hoping it's over. Banner's made friends with Julianne and Nicole, but she could use a few more, especially if I'm going to ask her to make Gold Haven her permanent home, preferably by moving in to my place.

I know what it's like to be an outsider here, and there were plenty of times I questioned my decision to come back rather than make a new start somewhere else. Banner doesn't have the roots that I do. She just has me.

Am I enough to keep her here?

For the rest of my drive, I rack my brain about how I can make Gold Haven out to be the best choice for her. Banner could go anywhere, but I want her tied here.

I put my thoughts on hold when I drive into the lot of Pro Interiors and park my truck near the door.

When I dropped the seats off on Monday, I headed home as quickly as possible. Today, I need to go over all the work to make sure it's exactly what I want for Boone's car. The guys here know who the end customer is, so I'm hoping they did a top-notch job.

The owner wasn't here last time, so when I approach the counter and see a different man with dark hair pulled into a short knot behind his head, I wonder if I'm finally going to meet him.

"Can I help you?" the man asks when I walk in.

"Logan Brantley. Here to pick up the interior pieces for the Olds 442 I'm redoing for Boone Thrasher."

His eyes light with recognition. He's definitely heard of me.

"You're the one who got his ass saved with a bunch of favors being pulled in. I'm Del. This is my place."

I'm not a fan of how he describes me, even though it's the truth. "Yeah, that's me."

"Sweet design, brother. You're lucky we were able to pull it off. I had people pulling all-nighters on it since you brought it in."

"I appreciate that. This is a big project for me, and my normal person couldn't handle it."

The man laughs. "Oh, I heard the whole story. Bowling fight and some injured female pride."

I jerk my head back in shock. *Banner*. "I guess you don't need me to explain then."

"I don't pull out all the stops in this place for no reason. Sounds like you've got your hands full with that woman. She must be a good one, because she made sure your ass was covered."

"She's the best there is."

Del nods. "I bet. You wanna see what we did? We just finished up an hour ago, and it's all waiting for you in the back."

"Hell yeah."

He waves me back, and I slide around the counter to follow him into the shop where a dozen people sit behind sewing machines designed specifically for upholstery. He leads me to a corner, where all the seats sit on canvas tarps.

"What do you think?"

The red-and-black seats with contrast stitching and brass-knuckle accents turned out better than I could have ever imagined.

"Holy shit. That's incredible."

"That's why we get the big bucks. Helps that your design didn't suck."

His "big bucks" comment seems off to me considering the price they quoted me could have been much higher and I would have paid it.

"I'll get a few guys to bag them up in plastic, and we'll load them in your truck for you."

"Appreciate it."

"You and I can settle up the bill, and you'll be on your way." Del walks back toward the counter, and I follow him. "You gotta let me know when you're going to be in town with the finished car. I want to make sure to get pictures for my marketing materials."

"Yeah, sure. This Saturday, you can see the Olds in all her glory."

"Glad your girl called, because there's no way anyone else could've pulled off this project but us on this short of notice. We're the top-of-the-line auto-interior experts for restoration in the South."

"Shit, it sounds like I might have to bring more of my business your way," I tell him as we reach the counter and I pull out my wallet. "What's the total damage?"

Del types something in on the computer. "Let me pull up this invoice and make sure. I can't remember off the top of my head. All I know is that your woman covered a chunk, so there's not much left for you."

Just like that, all the good feelings I had about this place crumble.

"What did you say?"

He looks up at me from the computer and then back down at the screen. "Never mind, man, that's not important."

"What the hell are you talking about? That my woman covered a chunk? She told me what the price was, and that was that." Suspicion and anger come to life.

Del hits a key, and the printer spits out an invoice. "Nothing. Forget I said anything."

I reach across the counter to snatch the paper off the printer tray.

The only amount on it is what I figured would be due. There's nothing about a deposit or any other payments being made. I don't know what Banner did, but it's going to be undone. We're going to have a come-to-Jesus talk about this.

I pull out my wallet and toss my company credit card on the counter. "You can charge me for all of it. And you're gonna tell me how much she paid, because she needs to get refunded."

"Dude, I wasn't supposed to say anything. I swore I wouldn't."

I wait in silence because the alternative will burn this bridge faster than a Hellfire missile strike.

Del finally speaks again. "Do you really think any shop would take on a project and have employees pull all-nighters and not charge you some kind of premium? Come on, man."

"How much?" I ask through my teeth.

"The rush fee was triple the normal cost. Your woman paid it so you only had to cover our regular price."

"So you're telling me I'm paying you a total of four times what you'd normally charge for this job? The regular price plus a triple rush fee?"

He nods.

"Fucking hell."

"We're booked out four months in advance right now, so we don't do shit like that unless it's worth our while."

"Refund her card and then charge me all of it." Fuck, this is going to set me back on the profit I figured I'd pull in from the job, but it has to be done.

Del hits a few more keys on the keyboard. "Unless you've got her card handy, I can't do that."

Fuck. "If she calls with the number, you'll refund it, though?"

He looks up. "Only if you're right there with another card to charge it to. I don't do this shit for free."

"Not a problem."

"Maybe this isn't my place, but you ever think about accepting her goodwill gesture and just move on? She pulled in favors to cover your ass, and you don't sound all that grateful about it."

The last thing I need is a lecture from a stranger. "I'm grateful; don't get me wrong. But I'm also the kind of man who pays for his own shit, regardless of how I got in that position."

Del shrugs and grabs my credit card off the counter to run it for the remaining amount. "Fair enough."

After I sign the receipt, we head outside where two of his guys are ready to load the seats into the back of my truck.

"Appreciate your help." I shake both guys' hands once they're finished and turn to Del. "Appreciate yours too."

"Don't be too hard on her. It was my fuckup that you

ever found out to begin with."

We shake hands, and when I release his, I respond. "Yeah, but she's the one who asked you not to tell me, and that ain't cool. I'll deal with that myself, though. Thanks again."

I climb into my truck and turn the key. As I'm pulling out of the parking lot, my first instinct is to pick up my phone and call Banner to ask her what the hell she was thinking, but this can wait until I see her.

It's a long ride home to Gold Haven.

TWENTY-NINE

Banner

I RUSH AROUND LOGAN'S KITCHEN, DARTING BETWEEN the oven and the stove and the microwave and the fridge, hoping like hell I can actually pull off my supposedly simple dinner of home-style baked pork chops, mashed potatoes, steamed broccoli, and cherry cobbler.

Women who do this every day should be rewarded with a boatload of medals, because it is *not* easy. The shopping, the prep, the planning, and sweet Jesus, the *timing*.

If Logan comes home late and all this turns to crap or ends up cold, I might sit down at the bar and cry into my wine.

Wine. Maybe that's the answer. I pour another glass of the red I picked up at the store, and take a sip. *Okay, I can do this. I feel good.*

At least until the kitchen timer goes off, and I have to scramble to remember which thing I was actually timing. The broccoli is last, so it has to be the potatoes.

A giant pot is boiling on the stove, and I pull up the recipe on my phone again and reread how to test to see if they're done.

Stabbing them with a fork doesn't seem all that hard. I attempt to stab into a potato on the top of the pile, but it evades me.

Shit.

Reaching for a big spoon, I fish a potato out and stab it. The fork slides in and out easily.

That means it's done, right?

I bet this is where people with normal families would be able to pick up the phone and call Mom for further instructions. But I don't have a normal family, and the only person I could call to ask would have been Mrs. Frances. A pang of sadness brings the burn of tears behind my eyes along with a reminder that I need to call Sofia and check in on both her and Jordana.

After I left New York, I decided there was no point in the apartment staying empty, so I asked if Sofia would live there with Ms. Jordy to house-sit for me. From her response, you would have thought she inherited the thirty million. All in all, the perfect solution.

Which reminds me: I need to talk to my financial adviser guy to make sure he took care of setting up payments to her as well.

Sofia refused to let me pay her for house-sitting and insisted that she didn't want to stop working with elderly people in the city who needed full-time in-home care, and I had to respect that decision. But that doesn't mean I can't put money in her bank account and tell her it's from Jordy's pet trust and she's entitled to it. I think Frau Frances would approve, so I'm doing it anyway.

I look back down at the potatoes and hope they're done.

I'm in the process of straining them in the sink and trying to avoid third-degree burns when another timer goes off.

Shit. Which one is that?

I dump a few potatoes into the sink by accident, but toss them back in the pot anyway before setting it down on a cold burner. *Whatever. I rinsed Logan's sink. It's fine. Five-second rule, right?*

I check my phone to see which timer is wailing now. The cobbler. It said something about needing to cool for an hour before eating. I return to the oven and open it. The red cherry glaze stuff that I bought, because there was no way I could make that filling from scratch, oozes down the side of the white dish and lands with a sizzle on the bottom of the oven.

Shit. That's going to be a mess.

I grab two pot holders and slide the dish out of the oven, then carefully set it on the counter with one of the pot holders shoved underneath.

Sweat beads on my forehead and neck as I stick my face in the oven again to assess the pork chops. Stuff is bubbling around them. That's quite literally all I can tell. A chef, I am not. The timer is still set for another fifteen minutes, so I hope, for the millionth time, that Logan gets here around when I calculated. A few minutes either way isn't going to ruin things, right?

I close the oven and grab my wineglass while I dig through the drawers for a meat thermometer. I've never used one in my life, but I don't want to take the chance of poisoning either of us with rare pork chops.

After draining the wineglass, I find the thermometer and locate a hand mixer to mash the potatoes. I don't know how other people do it, but I looked up *making mashed potatoes for idiots*, and it pulled up a super helpful site. I then had to google *potato ricer* and *food mill*, and came to the conclusion that Logan didn't have either. But he did have a good old-fashioned hand mixer, and after digging through more drawers, I found the little attachments.

I set out the milk and butter and pull my hair up into a bun. All I need is some gangster rap to fit my favorite meme. *I can handle this.*

I measure the milk and butter and wait until the pork chops only have seven minutes left before I get the broccoli steaming. Then I start mashing.

The mixer might be from 1972, given the avocado-green color and the racket it makes, but it mashes just fine. At least it does until someone taps me on the shoulder, and I scream and spin around, mixer still in hand.

Oh. Fuck.

Mashed potatoes fly *everywhere*, landing in globs, including right on Logan's face.

My heart pounding, I panic and push all the buttons on the top, which only turns up the speed, making an even bigger mess.

Logan reaches around me and yanks the cord out of the wall.

His long-sleeved black thermal shirt is covered in potato splatter, as are his face and hair. The dark look on his face doesn't signal good things for me.

"I'm so sorry. I didn't mean to—"

"Lie to me about how much the upholstery work was gonna cost, and let me walk into it thinking I got a great deal?"

Shit. I shove the mixer back in the pot with the pota-toes, and grab a towel.

"I just wanted to help. It was my fault that you couldn't use your regular lady anymore. You shouldn't have to pay that price. That was on me, so I fixed it."

Logan takes a deep breath and closes his eyes for a beat before he meets my gaze. "Was that upholstery for my business?"

"Yes, but—"

"Do I step in the middle of your business and do shit without asking you?"

"No, but—"

"I'm done with the buts, Banner. You've got more mon-ey than I'll ever make in a lifetime. I didn't ask you to throw it at my problems to make them go away. That's not how this thing between us works."

He takes the towel I'm holding and wipes the mashed potatoes off his face while I process his words. I understand where he's coming from, but he's missing the point.

"So you're saying if you pissed off the factory to the point they wouldn't make my product anymore unless you apologized, but I wouldn't let you apologize, you wouldn't pull out all the stops to figure out how to fix the problem? Or would you just let me deal with it myself and somehow be able to sleep at night?"

His hard expression softens. "I'd move mountains for you, Banner. I'd do anything in my power to make your life easier."

I was all fired up to throw down my next argument, but it fades away. Logan isn't just a good man, he's the best.

"Then how can you expect me to do any less for you? I

love you, Logan. I wouldn't just move mountains; I'd build ships to cross oceans if that's what it takes. That money is a tool, and if there's a time when I need to use it to make either or both of our lives easier, I'm going to do it."

Logan pulls me against his potato-spattered chest. "Jesus, woman. You make it fucking impossible to be mad at you when you say things like that."

The tension in my shoulders drains away and I pull my head back. "Even though I covered you in mashed potatoes?"

"Is that what you were making? I couldn't tell while it was flying at my face." He reaches out a hand, and before I can ask why, he brings it back to his mouth and sucks the mashed potatoes off his finger.

"They're not totally done."

His lips curl up into a smile. "But they're really fucking good."

I open my mouth to say something else, but my final timer goes off. "That's the pork chops and the broccoli."

Logan's eyes widen. "Damn, babe. You cooked a feast." He pauses and tilts his head to the side. "What's the occasion?"

I grin. "My favorite one—because I can."

Logan laughs and releases me to pull the pork chops from the oven.

THIRTY

Logan

I HAD A BIG SPEECH PREPARED ABOUT HOW I WASN'T going to let Banner spend her money on my business ever again, but I put it to rest when I realized something else.

This woman is a gift in my life, and although she might not do what's conventional, she acts with her whole heart, and it's hard to fault her for that.

Shit, it's hard to do anything more than fall deeper in love with her.

Plus, seeing her in my kitchen when I came home? Call me a caveman if you want, but I like it. I don't expect her to cook for me, but seeing she made the effort when she didn't have to was a good surprise.

An even better surprise? The food is phenomenal. I don't have to pretend to want more, because my second helping goes down just as quick as the first.

"You know there's cherry cobbler too, so you might want to save room for dessert."

My fork stills in midair. "Did you say cherry cobbler?"

She nods. "I haven't tried it, so I don't know how it turned out—"

Banner trails off when I stuff the last bite of pork chop into my mouth and stand up to move around the bar.

"Whoa, you would've thought I told you I buried the keys to a Ferrari in that thing. I didn't even mention the vanilla ice cream in the freezer."

I glance back at her as I reach for bowls. "I'm gonna get fat living with you if you keep cooking like this."

Banner's eyes go wide, and I realize what I just said.

"We're not exactly living together." Her voice is quiet.

"For all intents and purposes, we are. Might as well make it official."

"You . . . you want to live with me? Like move in together?"

I lower the bowls to the counter and turn to face her, my sweet tooth on hold for a moment. "Are you seriously asking that question?"

Banner nods. "I seriously am."

"You think there's a morning where I don't want to wake up with you in my bed? You think there's a night where I don't want to fall asleep with you in my arms?"

Her eyes turn shiny. "Are you sure?"

I come back around the bar and stop in front of her. "You're it for me, Banner. The one. I'd given up on finding the perfect woman for me, but you showed me I hadn't been looking in the right place. Who knew I had to go all the way to New York City? I'm not stopping with you moving in. There's a lot more I want, but I'm not pushing you until you've had a chance to come around to my way of thinking."

"Really?"

I nod. "Really."

She blinks those tears away just before I slide my hand into her hair and cover her lips with mine. When I pull back, she's staring at me like she's never seen me before.

"What, Bruce?"

"You're the best man I've ever known, and you're *mine*."

"All yours and no one else's."

"You better let me try the cherry cobbler first, just in case it's terrible. I'm not chancing it now."

My laugh bounces off the walls of the kitchen. "You could give me food poisoning, and I wouldn't change my mind about a damn thing."

Banner presses three fingers over my lips. "Don't say it. I forgot to check the pork with the meat thermometer. I hope we don't get trichinosis."

I kiss the back of her fingers before stepping away. "We'll be fine."

Back in the kitchen, I load up two bowls with heaping mounds of cherry cobbler, then find the ice cream in the freezer and add a big scoop to each.

It's fucking amazing.

When we finish, Banner and I clean up the pota-to-spattered mess of the kitchen together. I pat my stomach, which is as full as I can remember it being since last Thanksgiving. "I'm going to have to up my gym sessions to five days a week if you're going to keep cooking like that."

Banner shoots me a look. "When do you have time to go to the gym anyway?"

"Why do you think I get up so early? I hit it in the mornings, three days a week. You think I look like this from wrenching on cars?"

"I didn't give it any thought at all beyond appreciating every single inch of it."

The inches I want her to appreciate are sitting up and taking notice.

Once the last dish is in the dishwasher, I pull her back against my chest. "You know, you might have had a good reason to step in and help me out with the upholstery place, but next time, you need to talk to me about it first, babe."

"I can manage that." She pauses. "Does that mean you're still pissed?"

I squeeze her against me. "I couldn't stay pissed at you if I tried."

Her ass wiggles against my crotch. "But you still might want to punish me for being a naughty girl, right?"

I crane my head sideways to look down at her face. Her expression is filled with pure mischief. "I think you want me to punish you for being a naughty girl."

Her entire body tenses. "I mean, you should make sure I learn my lesson."

My dick is no longer sitting up and taking notice, but instead is rock hard and ready to punch through my jeans.

"Is that right?" I step back and slide a hand down her back to grip her ass. "If I turn this red, you'll remember better next time?"

She presses back into my touch, and I know that my girl isn't just amazing. She's perfect.

"Maybe."

I set her away from me. "I want to see you in the bedroom, laid out over the bed, everything off but your bra and panties." When she doesn't move immediately, I give her ass a smack. "Now."

Banner bolts away, already pulling off her shirt before she leaves the kitchen.

In fact, I follow her trail of discarded clothes two minutes later as I walk toward the bedroom. I pick up each piece and drop them inside the doorway. She's exactly where I asked her to be, all laid out and waiting for me.

I reach for the back of my shirt and strip it over my head before unbuttoning my jeans and shoving them off.

"You were a bad girl, weren't you, Banner?" I ask as I step closer to her. Her ass lifts in anticipation of what's coming.

"Yes. Very bad."

Fuck. I love that she wants to play these games with me.

"So I'm going to have to punish you to remind you to always tell me the whole truth."

"Yes. I need some help remembering."

One more step, and I'm beside the bed and within touching distance. I trail two fingers down her spine to the top of her thong.

"I think a fitting punishment is pulling these flimsy panties off you and then spanking your ass until you tell me you'll never do it again."

"Mmm. Yes."

"Then what am I waiting for?" I land the first strike, and immediately cup her ass cheek and soothe what I just stung. It's already heating under my hand.

"You're moving your stuff in tomorrow. We can tell

Holly that we'll keep an eye on the house together, but I want you here all the time."

Banner turns her head and looks up at me over her shoulder. "I think she'll understand."

"I think she will too."

THIRTY-ONE

Logan

I PICKED UP THE OLDS 442 FROM THE PAINT SHOP ON Thursday, and they came through in a big way. Everything is perfect, right down to the red pinstripes. Jock and Rick finished installing the seats and shining up every inch of the interior just as the clock flipped to five p.m.

Projects like this are what I live for. And even with all the hurdles, it turned out like a boss.

I might be getting ahead of myself, but Boone Thrasher is going to be a happy man. His custom shifter came in yesterday, and now the knob reads *BT* in black letters on the top, intertwined with brass knuckles.

"I know someone's gotta take it for a test-drive, and boss, you deserve an early night—" Rick says, and I hold up a hand.

"No way in hell is anyone test-driving this beast but me." I reach into my pocket for my wallet. "You two worked your asses off, and I appreciate it. Go have a few beers on me." I hold out a fifty.

Jock steps up and snags it from my hand. "You ain't gotta tell us twice. Come on, Rick. We can race to Pints and Pins."

Rick grumbles and sends one more longing look at the Olds before nodding to me. "Someday I'm gonna do one of these cars for myself. Breaks a little piece of my heart every time we finish one and have to let it go."

His words bring up something I've been thinking about. There's a woman I know who was born to drive a cherry-red convertible, and because she's as unique as it gets, it can't be something you can just drive off the lot. As soon as we get back from Nashville, I'm going to be on the lookout for Banner's new car, a project I'm happy to take on to surprise her. She also doesn't know she's going to Nashville this weekend, but I'll tell her tonight. She's probably dying to get out of Gold Haven for a minute and into a real city with a Starbucks.

The guys head out, and I hear their trucks fire up in the lot. I pull out my phone to call Banner, but it's already buzzing with Boone Thrasher's name on the screen.

"Hey, Boone."

"You're getting down to the wire, and I've got a big thing planned for that car. Tell me it's done, Brantley."

"It's done."

"Thank fuck. This shit is gonna be epic. My girl will be there, and I'm gonna surprise her by asking her to marry me, then drive right offstage in the car so we can break it in right. I bought the ring yesterday and everything."

"Holy shit, man. Congratulations. Wow." If I remember right, Boone's girlfriend is another country singer. A tiny thing who looks and sounds more like a pop star. I prefer

Holly's brand of country, and that's without the personal bias.

"Wow is right. Never fuckin' thought I'd see the day I'd want to tie myself to a woman, but she's the first one who's ever understood what this life is like and can hack it with me."

"That's great. I'm glad the car is ready so you can make it happen."

"You doin' all right? You bringin' that city girl with you so I can show you both a good time? I've got all-access passes for the both of you, and a suite where you can crash so you don't have to drive back after the show. Press conference and all the classic-car mags are going to be showing up Saturday morning starting at noon, so I can make an appearance and tell them all about the project before I have to get in the zone for the show and start worrying about sound checks and that shit. And fuck, I'm proposing Saturday night. Jesus Christ. I can't even believe it myself."

"We'll be there tomorrow with the car. I'll load it up in the morning in the enclosed trailer, and we can bring it right to the stadium for you so you don't have to worry about anything."

"Perfect. I'll tell my guy to make sure that you've got a reservation for tomorrow night too. Thanks for pulling through, man. Not everyone can be true to their word these days, but I knew you would. Holly had good things to say, and she knows her shit when it comes to people."

"I appreciate the vote of confidence. I aim to please."

"You better get ready to expand that shop of yours. My buddies are already thinking about using you, and they haven't even seen the car yet."

A smile stretches over my face. "I'm ready for whatever they want."

"Perfect. Now I gotta go meet my future father-in-law for dinner and ask him if I can propose to his baby girl. Fuck. I haven't been this nervous about anything since my first sold-out show."

"How could he possibly say no?" I ask, hoping I'm right. I'm actually surprised as hell that Boone is sharing all this with me.

"You're right. I'm Boone Fucking Thrasher. I got this. See you and the ride tomorrow," he says before he hangs up.

More than ever, I'm really glad that it all came together. Now I just need to take the car on a nice and easy test-drive with Banner and do a few last-minute checks on it before I load it up in the trailer in the morning.

I tap my screen a few times to bring up our last text.

LOGAN: *Wanna meet me at the shop? We're going for a ride.*

MY WOMAN: *Did someone say ride? I'm so there. Give me a few to get ready. I've been up to my elbows in dicks all day.*

I laugh and tuck my phone back in my pocket before heading to the overhead door to open it. As soon as I step outside, Julianne waves from the window of Cut a Bitch, and I wave back. She comes out, walks across the street, and sticks her head inside.

"Oh my hell. Is this Boone Thrasher's car? Holy shit. It is *hot*."

"Sure is. He's gonna see it tomorrow for the first time."

"You mean he's gonna get laid tomorrow in it for the first time, because that's what a badass like him would do."

"Not going there with you."

"Well, I'm just sayin'. You gonna drive it?"

"Waitin' on Banner to get here."

"Can I talk to you about one thing before you go?"

"What's that?"

"I was down at the county building renewing my DBA, and that reporter chick was there pulling all kinds of property-tax records and searching deeds and stuff."

"So?"

"I heard her tell someone at Home Cookin' earlier today that she's been interviewing lots of people, and she mentioned you as being particularly helpful. You better believe a lot of people were shocked by that."

"I didn't tell her shit."

"You might want to set the record straight. Now everyone thinks you must've given her some kind of big tip, because she says she's close to breaking the case."

"I don't have time for this crap. I've got a business to run, and I'm sure as shit not letting her get in my way."

"Whatever you say, Logan. But I thought you should know."

"I'll keep that in mind."

"Have you heard anything else about Nicole? I asked Cody when I cut his hair, but of course he wouldn't say shit to me."

I shake my head. I've been so caught up in my deadline, I haven't had a chance to track Nicole down. "She's been scarce; that's all I know."

"I saw her down at the bowling alley working, but it

was a quiet night and everyone seemed to be staying at their tables and waiting for Rosie to take orders rather than going up to the bar. It's like the court of public opinion has already passed judgment on her, and it wasn't favorable."

"She didn't do shit. You and I both know it."

Julianne shrugs. "Just because she's our friend doesn't mean she's a saint, Logan. Sweet job on the car. It's nice to see another one of our own making good again, especially with all this bullshit happening. Catch ya later."

With a wave, she strides out of the garage, and I'm left wondering if this town will ever be the same.

THIRTY-TWO

Banner

I TRIED TO HURRY; I REALLY DID. BUT HONESTLY, I didn't have a clue what I should wear to go ride around in Boone Thrasher's badass car. It brings a smile to my face to know that it wouldn't be nearly so badass if my man hadn't made it that way.

And we already took it to Brown Town . . .

Flashes of what it was like to be bent over the hood of the car while Logan powered into me from behind flip through my brain. Damn, that was hot.

If I'm not careful, I might throw myself at Logan as soon as I see him, and I know with the new paint job, there won't be any more action happening on the 442. It's a sad fact, but one I'll find a way to live with.

I stop at the back door to slide on my boots and complete what I've come to think of as my Gold Haven uniform—skinny jeans, knee-high boots, and a black top. I stood in the closet forever debating between this and my super-short skirt I wore the other night. Should I have gone with the skirt? Maybe, but I've wasted enough time as it is, and Logan has to be chomping at the bit to take this car for a spin.

The clock on the dash of my rental car tells me I'm running further behind than I should be. I told him a few minutes, but it's been closer to an hour. Maybe I should offer up some road head to apologize for my tardiness so he won't hold it against me.

Then I'd have two things to tell Boone Thrasher about his precious new car. *Hmm, I consider that a point in favor of road head.*

I flip the radio station to the local country channel, a new taste I've acquired, and as though destined, one of Boone's songs is playing.

He's got this gravelly voice that instantly conjures thoughts of driving down backcountry roads in a pickup truck. All the things he describes were completely foreign to me only two months ago, and now they've become part of my everyday life. Life in a small country town is a completely different proposition than living in New York.

Boone delivers one hell of a performance, and Logan doesn't know it yet, but I'm already planning on being a stowaway when he goes to deliver the car tomorrow so I can meet this guy in person.

I slow at the stop sign about two hundred feet before the blinking light at the Four Corners, and a blast drowns out the song. My car is at a complete stop, but it shakes anyway.

The percussion seems to echo, and I freeze. *Did the whole town just explode?*

Jarring myself out of my momentary paralysis, I scan the buildings in front of me. From behind a stand of huge oak trees, a raging fire meets a cloud of black smoke forming in the sky.

Logan's shop is on the other side of those trees.

I floor my accelerator until the source of the smoke comes into view. Flames lick into the sky from the garage.

Where I'm meeting Logan.

Oh my God. His truck is parked near the Dumpsters, but there's no sign of him, or of Boone's car.

"No!" I scream, my voice shaking as I jerk my wheel to the side. My tire collides with the curb, but I don't care as I slam it into park.

I jump out of the car and run toward the inferno, heat already warming my face.

"Stop! Don't!"

A man reaches out and grabs me around the waist, dragging me back when my heels connect with the pavement to keep moving forward.

"No!" My voice doesn't sound like me. It's ragged. Desperate. Terrified.

"Get back. Everyone, get back! The gas tanks are gonna blow!" the man yells as he pulls me around the side of the post office. "Take cover!"

I don't know who he's yelling at, but all I want is to free myself from his iron grip.

"Let me go! I have to get to him! Logan's in there." I whip my head around to fight against the man, but he's too strong.

"You wanna get killed? We gotta get back." He stops once we're safe behind the post office, and the percussion of another explosion rocks the ground.

"Get down!" He pushes me to my knees and covers me

with his body.

Screams split the air, and sirens wail in the distance.

It's chaos. Complete and utter chaos. And only one thought is running through my head on repeat: *I have to get to Logan.*

I crawl out from under the man to stand, but freeze when I see the blaze reaching higher into the sky. My eyes burn, and tears stream down my face.

A door slams beside me, startling me and dragging me out of my disjointed thoughts.

"Oh my fucking God! What the hell just happened?" Julianne's voice cuts through the static in my head as she shuts the back door of Cut a Bitch. "I was in the basement. My front window is blown out. Logan's shop is . . . rubble." She whispers the last word as I run toward her.

"Where is he?" I demand. "Did you see him?"

I run to the corner of the building with Julianne on my heels. The fire is so intense, it heats my face as soon as I step beyond the protection of the concrete walls.

"I . . . I just talked to him about twenty minutes ago. He was waiting for you in the garage." Her voice trembles as if she wishes she was saying anything but the words coming out of her mouth.

"No!"

Sheer agony rips through me. I slap a hand over my chest, trying to stop the pain, and wonder why there isn't a gaping hole in my chest where my heart was ripped out.

"I'm so sorry," she whispers.

"He couldn't have been—" I choke on the words and start again. "He wasn't—"

"I'm so sorry," Julianne repeats, shaking her head. "I'm

so sorry."

Wailing sirens come closer and pierce the buzzing in my ears.

"Oh my God. I'm going to be sick." I jerk away from Julianne, pressing a hand to the wall of the building as I empty my stomach on the pitted asphalt before falling backward onto my ass.

Julianne joins me on the ground and wraps her arms around me, and together we rock back and forth. I don't know how long we stay like that before someone comes around the building and starts barking out orders.

"You need to get back. We need everyone at least two hundred feet away. This isn't safe."

"Jesus, Cody," Julianne says. "What the fuck just happened?"

Through the tears blurring my eyes, I see the man issuing orders. The cop. He knows Logan.

"Where's Logan?" I demand. "Is he out there? Please tell me you saw him."

The cop's expression is grim. "I haven't seen him. That's not to say he's not out here somewhere. It's a fucking madhouse, but I need you both to go back behind the post office and stay out of harm's way. We're not taking any chances with this shit."

I'm on my knees, my hand on his jeans, as I beg him, "Please. Find him. I can't lose him. Please."

The cop crouches down to wrap an arm around me, and helps me to my feet. "Look, I know we haven't been formally introduced, but I'm Cody, ma'am, and I need you to come on around the back of the building so I can make sure you're safe."

I slap a hand to his chest. "Why are you worried about us? Logan—" My voice breaks again as he half carries me around the back of the building where the man who pulled me back from the fire is still standing.

"Did you see that shit?" the man asks.

Cody releases me, and Julianne glues herself to my side.

"No," Cody says, "but I heard it. Did you see it? We're gonna need witnesses so I can figure out what happened."

"I saw part of it," the man said. "I was in my car, getting ready to leave. I thought I smelled something funny, and then I heard the explosion and saw the flames."

"I didn't see it," Julianne says, snuffling back her tears. "I just felt it. Thought the entire building was going to come down on my head."

"I saw the fire," I say. "Felt the blast. I tried to get closer, but he—" I point to the guy standing a few feet away. "He stopped me."

Cody nods, and the man who grabbed me speaks again. "I saw her start running, so I jumped out of my car and pulled her back. I knew the service station tanks were gonna blow. Didn't want anyone else gettin' hurt, Cody."

At the words *anyone else*, a sob escapes my throat, and my body shakes uncontrollably.

"It's okay, Lonnie. You did what you needed to do." Cody's gaze lands on me again. "Shit. You going into shock? Ambulance is already on its way."

"Logan," I whisper, my voice destroyed.

Julianne knows what I'm trying to say, and finishes my thought. "He was inside."

Cody's face falls. "You're fucking kidding me."

Julianne shakes her head. "Inside. Waiting—" She cuts

off her word as she looks at me.

Cody rubs a hand down his face. "Well, there's nothing you can do here right now. We need everyone to stay back so the firefighters can do their job. The gas pumps made this a hell of a lot worse." More sirens approach, and this time they're coming from the ambulance. "Let's get you checked out, ma'am," he says to me.

I wrap both arms around my chest, rocking on my heels as I shake my head. "No. I'm not going anywhere. I'm staying right here." If he tries to move me, I'll scream.

"I'm real sorry, ma'am. But Logan would want me to make sure—"

"Shut up! Don't talk about him!" I'm nearly hysterical, but I don't care. If a doctor were to tell me I'm dying right now, I'd believe him. I've never felt this kind of pain crushing down on me.

"I gotta go make sure the perimeter is solid. Julianne, can you make sure she stays back?"

I hate that he's talking about me like I'm not here, but I don't have the energy to argue.

"Of course. I got her."

"Lonnie, if you could write down everything you remember right now to give me as an official statement, I'd appreciate it."

The man nods. "I can do that. No problem."

An unwelcome voice joins the conversation.

"Oh my word, Officer. What in the world just happened?" Emmy Harris rushes over to join our small group. "I was taking inventory in the back when I heard it all. Do we need to evacuate? Was it some kind of chemical explosion? Is it even safe to be here?"

"You should go back to the restaurant, Emmy. Make sure everyone stays inside. Maybe get some coffee going for the firefighters. It's gonna be a few hours before this thing is under control."

"Of course. Anything I can do to help. Do we know if anyone was hurt?" she asks, sending another slice of pain ripping through my body.

"Logan was inside," Julianne whispers.

Emmy's hand flies to her face, and her eyes immediately fill with tears. "No. That's not possible. He couldn't have been—"

"We're not going to be able to tell for sure until the fire is out and the chief can walk through the structure," Cody says.

We all know what he's not saying. That the fire chief, Logan's friend, has to look for a body to be sure.

My chest feels like it's collapsing under a thousand-pound weight, and sobs rack my body.

THIRTY-THREE

Logan
Fifteen minutes earlier

TODAY JUST HASN'T BEEN MY DAY. SERIOUSLY, sometimes I wonder how in the hell my employees manage to do a damned thing right when Rick can't remember any of his shit when he leaves the shop.

Julianne's words stay with me as I head back into the garage to grab a chamois to wipe down the Olds 442 one more time before Banner gets here. That's when I see Rick's wallet sticking out from the top of his toolbox, which he also forgot to close and lock up in his haste to leave.

I don't blame him for being in a hurry. Both he and Jock have busted their asses working on this car and the other repair jobs we've had come in.

I owe Holly one hell of a thank-you for talking this place up to Boone, because this is going to change everything. Just goes to show that life really does revolve around who you know.

I could get pissed at that reality, or I can accept it. I choose the second. I may never be on Banner's financial level, what with her inheritance, but at least I'm not some hick who looks like he's just with her as a sugar mama. My pride wouldn't allow it.

With the chamois and wallet in hand, I check the time. She said a few minutes, but I've learned that in Banner speak, that could be an hour. Might as well fire up the old girl and put her through her paces.

There's nothing quite like the rumble of a big-block engine, and when I turn the key, I'm anticipating the vibrations that will roll through my body. Instead, all I get is a click.

Fuck. My stomach sinks.

I pull the hood release, hop out of the car, and go around to check. It only takes a few minutes before I realize what the problem is. Battery is still disconnected. I hook it back up and shut the hood.

Do not fuck with me, world. This needs to be perfect.

I hold my breath the second time I turn the key.

Thank God.

The rumble of the big block rolls through my body, and a sense of accomplishment comes along with it.

I did this.

After I shift into gear, I press down on the accelerator and let her roll out of the garage. Adrenaline dumps into my veins, and I decide to say *fuck it* about putting the door down. I'll be back quick, and the nosy people of Gold Haven are enough of a security system for me.

I keep the growl of the exhaust low until I'm a quarter mile away from the Four Corners where the speed limit changes from thirty-five to fifty-five. Then I open her up.

My laugh is lost in the snarl of the engine as the

speedometer climbs. I can't wait to do this with Banner in the seat beside me.

Life is fucking good.

It took longer than I thought to drop off Rick's wallet at the bowling alley. Every single person who was there for the Thursday-night bowling league came out to admire Boone Thrasher's new beauty of a car.

If I had to make a bet, I'd say that more than one guy went back inside and started searching for his own project. They might not be able to afford my prices for the entire thing, but I think I just started a muscle-car revolution.

I'm extra careful in the gravel parking lot as I pull out, not wanting to chip the pristine paint job. It takes all the restraint I have not to do a burn out once I'm on pavement. Knowing that Boone is gonna want to tear up his own tires is the only thing that keeps me from it.

I shift into a lower gear at the sound of sirens up ahead as I close in on downtown. It's not an uncommon occurrence, given the sheer number of old folks having heart-attack scares. But as I get closer, the wail is louder and louder.

Fuck, I hope it's not Mrs.—

My thought cuts off when my gaze locks on flames climbing into the darkening sky just beyond the tree line.

My shop.

Banner.

Fuck.

No longer concerned about the tires, I floor it, and the engine roars as the car speeds toward a barricade blocking off the Four Corners intersection ahead. An inferno engulfs the painted cinder-block walls of my shop, leaving nothing visible but evil orange flames and thick black smoke.

Banner.

No!

I can't fucking lose her.

I remember the day I got the call that my ma was dead. I shed tears because that's what you do when you lose your last remaining family member. But this is nothing like that, even though it hurt like hell to know Ma killed herself with that needle in her vein.

Pain claws through me.

This is all my fault. I'm the only reason Banner's here, the reason she's at my shop. The reason she's still in Gold Haven. Fuck, I don't deserve anything as perfect as her in my life, because I can't keep it that way.

Cars have stopped everywhere, turning the road into a parking lot, and there's no way I can get through. Fury and rage have me whip the wheel to the left and cut down a side street, determined to get around them.

My heart thunders in my chest, keeping tempo with the rumble of the engine. Sweat coats my palms as I grip the steering wheel tighter.

I offer everything I own—and even things I don't—to every higher power in existence if there's some way she can be safe.

Blinding, instinctive fear grips my chest like a vise and crushes the breath from my lungs as I tear into the parking lot behind the pharmacy and the post office, where a crowd is gathered behind.

Up ahead, around the corner of the building, Banner's rental is parked.

No. Fuck. No.

My body shakes in my seat as I slam on the brakes without a care for the car, and yank open the door to run toward the blaze. To run toward her.

My feet hit the pavement, and I sprint.

"Logan? Oh my God!"

It's Julianne's voice, not the one I desperately want to hear. My gaze locks on her—and the woman next to her.

"Banner!"

THIRTY-FOUR

Banner

I BARELY HAVE MY FEET UNDER ME BEFORE I FLY TOWARD him, dodging the outstretched arms of the cop who would keep me away from Logan.

"Logan!"

He charges in my direction. "You're okay! Sweet fucking Christ. Don't you ever scare me like that. I thought you—"

My body slams into his, and Logan's arms wrap around me. "I thought you were inside. Oh my God. Julianne told me you were inside. I thought you were gone." Tears spill from my eyes onto his shirt, soaking the cotton fabric.

"No. Jesus Christ, I thought you were in there. Scared the shit out of me." He squeezes me so tight, I can barely breathe, and it's the best feeling in the world.

"Thank God you're okay."

Julianne and Emmy come toward us, but I don't care about anything except for the fact that Logan is alive and holding me.

He lifts his head and looks over my shoulder,

presumably at Cody. "What the fuck happened?"

I turn sideways to see the cop's face as he answers.

"I have no clue. But you need to stay back until they get this put out. Where the hell were you? Julianne said you were inside."

"Rick forgot his wallet, so I took it over to Pints and Pins."

Julianne punches Logan in the shoulder. "I didn't see you leave, you dumbass. I thought you were in there! I told Banner you were!"

Logan grips me even tighter when another sob escapes my lips. "Well, I wasn't."

"Oh my God, I can't believe you're okay. We all thought—" Emmy's voice breaks off.

Logan steps us around the edge of the post office so we can see what's left of the building, and the others follow. Foam covers the walls that remain standing as the firemen continue to fight the blaze.

It's a lost cause. No one has to announce that there will be nothing left, because it's perfectly clear.

"What the hell happened?" he asks again, and this time, someone answers.

"Trying to figure that out right now. I got the call and came down. Fully involved structure fire. Chemical hazards." Cody pauses. "I hate to have to ask you this, but you weren't cooking meth inside, were you? Or one of your guys?"

"Hell no." Logan spits out the words. "Fuck no," he adds for extra emphasis.

"No cigarettes left burning? Any kind of torch?"

Logan shakes his head. "No one smokes in the shop.

The torches were off. It doesn't make any fucking sense."

"Buildings don't just blow up, Logan. I don't have to tell you that."

"No shit. But I don't have a clue how it happened."

"It's lucky you weren't inside. How long ago did you leave?" the cop asks.

"I don't know, maybe fifteen, twenty minutes ago?"

"It's also pretty damn convenient that the car you just restored wasn't inside."

There's something in Cody's tone that I don't like, and apparently Logan doesn't either.

"What the fuck are you trying to say? That somehow I made this happen?" Logan's voice drops to a rough whisper. "Because there's no fucking way I had a goddamned thing to do with this. That shop is my business. My future."

"I'm just doing my job, and my training says money is always the best motive. And in this case, your insurance money."

"I didn't fucking have anything to do with it. I had two customers' cars inside, and shit I'll never be able to replace."

"But you know you're gonna have money coming in from insurance to cover it all for you."

Logan drops his arm from around my shoulders. "I can't fucking believe you'd bring that up right now. I didn't have a damned thing to do with this."

The fire chief breaks away from the men fighting the fire and strides toward us.

"Jesus fucking Christ, man. They told you were inside."

Logan releases me to hug the other man. "Fuck, Granger. I don't know if today is my lucky day or the unluckiest day I've ever had."

"You're breathing and not a charred corpse, so there's that. I gotta get back up there, but fuck, it's good to see you." Granger steps back and replaces his headgear, but before I can speak, Emmy chimes in.

"I'm so glad you're okay. I think my heart about stopped when I thought . . . well, never mind that now. I'm gonna get back to the restaurant and try to calm people down again. Granger, if any of you need coffee or water, it's on the house. I'll start brewing some now."

"Appreciate it, Emmy." Granger walks backward. "We got all hands on deck to put this one out."

"Me too," Cody says before striding away. Over his shoulder, he adds, "Logan, I don't need to tell you this, but don't go anywhere anytime soon. We're gonna have a bunch of questions for you."

"Jesus, what a clusterfuck," Julianne whispers.

"My fucking shop is gone."

"I'm sorry, babe. So sorry. But I'm so glad you're okay." I sniffle and tears fall again. "Don't you ever make me think you're dead again. I will seriously kill you myself."

Logan crushes me to his chest. "You scared the shit out of me too. I thought you could've been inside. Jesus. What a disaster."

I look at the car standing a few feet away, still running. "It's a miracle you weren't."

"Thank Rick's forgetfulness."

"You better believe I will. I'm going to give every woman he dates a vibrator. It's the least I can do."

"I'll leave you two alone," Julianne says. "I gotta go track down some plywood for my front window. Blast shattered it."

Logan looks from me to her. "Call the lumberyard and tell them to put it on my account. Explain what happened, and that you need it delivered tonight so you can actually leave your shop."

She nods and pulls out her phone before walking away to make the call.

I look up at Logan. "Cody said you can't go anywhere, but you gotta get the car to Nashville tomorrow."

"And I will. We will. You're coming with me. This world could be headed straight for hell, but I wouldn't let it stop me from delivering that car on time. Especially not after I talked to Boone tonight and told him it's ready to go."

"But what about Cody?"

Logan thinks for a few moments before responding. "Whatever questions they have aren't going to change the fact that I have a job to do. They'll get to the bottom of it, and I'll clean up the mess. But my business isn't gonna be worth much if I can't deliver on my word to Boone Thrasher."

"This timing sucks."

"Sure does, but there's not a damn thing we can do about it."

I lay my head on his chest, the acrid scent of smoke now clinging to both of us. "I'm sorry."

He presses a kiss to my forehead. "There's nothing for you to be sorry about. You and I are both okay, and at the end of the day, that's all that matters. Everything else can be replaced with money. There's no way in hell I could ever replace you, Banner." He pauses. "I've never felt fear as blinding as I did when I saw those flames from over the post office. In my gut, I knew it was coming from my shop, and I thought my worst nightmare was coming true."

I don't have to ask what his worst nightmare is because I already know. *Losing me.*

"I thought I was going to die when Julianne told me you were inside."

He brings me close to his chest again. "Like I'd ever leave you without a fight. Never."

"What are we going to do now?" I ask.

"For now, we wait. Tomorrow, we're driving to Nashville to deliver this car before anything else can happen."

THIRTY-FIVE

Logan

I T'S A LONG NIGHT OF WAITING IN THE PARKING LOT. Emmy Harris sets up a buffet on the sidewalk out in front of Home Cookin' to feed the firefighters as they continue to battle flare-ups. I've listened to Granger talk about putting out fires before, and I've even ridden along on a few training calls to watch, but it's nothing like watching them fight the blaze in my shop.

Before Banner, I would have said that I lost everything that mattered in there. But not anymore. As long as I have her, I've got everything I need. Everything else is replaceable.

I don't have a clue how long it's going to take me to rebuild, or how much money I'm going to lose, but knowing what I could have lost puts it all in perspective.

John Grove, the owner of the gas station that was connected to my shop, has been standing out front yelling at firemen since he got here. He's been an absentee owner for years, paying managers to work the station while he sits back and collects money. His retirement just went up in flames, and he's not handling it well at all.

Gossip is already spreading all over the place, and it doesn't help that Memphis Lockwood filmed a segment standing in the road in front of what used to be my business. The top three choices of speculation I've heard are that I burned it down for insurance money, or someone burned it down because they heard I was helping her, or it was an accident.

I know it wasn't the first option, and I have no idea which to pick out of the other two choices. Police Chief Timmons also made an appearance, shooing gawkers back from the perimeter and telling people to go home.

The residents of Gold Haven rarely have anything this exciting happen, and several brought coolers and lawn chairs to watch the spectacle rather than follow directions and go home.

Life in a small town, I suppose.

The lumberyard brought enough plywood to board up the busted or cracked windows of the post office, the hair salon, and the pharmacy. The fact that my business caused this kind of collateral damage is giving me heartburn, but Julianne at least has said that she's not going to hold it against me.

Even if she did, there's not a thing I could do about it.

I rack my brain to figure out the cause, but come up blank. What Julianne told me right before she left, about Memphis telling people I helped her out with the investigation, keeps running through my mind.

It's an unsettling thought, but someone might have tried to kill me. I can't say anything to Banner because she'll freak the fuck out, and probably try to hire security for me or something.

The townspeople start to drift away after Emmy closes up the buffet and the fire is finally out. It's been almost six hours.

Banner and I sit on a bench in front of the post office, watching but not speaking. There's not much to say.

Granger crosses the road and ducks under the yellow police tape set up as a perimeter. "Hey, I think we finally got it all. I'm going to take a look inside. If you want to suit up, you can come too."

I rise from the bench. "Stay here, babe. Or better yet, go inside with Julianne for a bit."

"But—"

"You're not setting foot in that shop, Banner."

"Damn right she's not," Granger adds. "It's too danger-ous for her."

Banner shuts her mouth, even though I know she wants to argue the point. "Fine. I'll go inside."

I press another kiss to her forehead and wait for her to slip into Cut a Bitch before I follow Granger to the fire truck and suit up in the extra set of gear. Once I'm finished, he waves me toward the building and we step through what used to be the door.

The steel beams that comprised the building are ex-posed now that the drywall is completely burned away. The waiting room is indistinguishable as we slosh through foamy insulation and metal shards into the shop area.

Granger points to a corner near the back door to the shop. The old-as-hell porcelain toilet is cracked but recog-nizable. "Looks like it started in the bathroom. The burn marks tell me it was chemical."

"What the hell? The bathroom?"

We skirt through the skeletons of two burned-out customer cars and the remains of my hydraulic lifts to get there.

Granger crouches to the floor and feels around. "I know you're not going to want to hear this, but it's got all the markings of a meth-lab fire. I gotta tell Cody and notify the state so they can send investigators out. We shouldn't be in here."

I follow him back through the path of destruction out what used to be one of the overhead doors. Once outside, I rip off my mask.

"That's fucking impossible. Neither Jock nor Rick was cookin' meth in my bathroom, and I sure as fuck wasn't either."

Granger shrugs. "I gotta be unbiased here, so I'm telling you what my training says. The signs are all there; they were just buried under the rest of the chemical elements you had present."

"Then someone set this up. It's no fucking accident."

Granger's mouth settles into a grim line. "I think you're right. It might not be an accident, but it was definitely some kind of setup, if you truly don't believe it was Jock or Rick."

"I'd bet my life on it."

"Well, buddy, then you've made an enemy who wants to make it look like you're cookin' meth."

Cody cuts through the crowd to stand beside Granger. "What do you think? Timmons is up my ass, wanting information."

Granger tells him everything he just said to me, including the fact that this doesn't look like it was an accident.

"This shit is escalating. We need someone with means, motive, and opportunity."

I'm racking my brain to figure that out. "Julianne was there, but there's no way it was her."

"I don't think we should be ruling anyone out at this point," Cody replies.

"I'll go give Timmons a report," Granger interjects. "It'll get him off your ass at least, and let him know I'm making a call to the state. They'll be down tomorrow morning to take a look and start their investigation."

"I know you said not to leave town, but everything I've got left of my business is riding on me delivering that car to Boone Thrasher in Nashville. It's not something I'm pawning off to anyone else either."

Cody meets my stare. "I'm telling you not to leave town, Logan, but what you do with that order is up to you."

"Stop being a hard-ass, Cody. You know you'd do the same," Granger argues.

"If Chief Timmons comes looking for you tomorrow and can't find you, that's not on me."

"Like he works on Fridays or weekends if he can help it. He's too busy drinking, and sleeping his way through the women in this town."

I jerk my gaze to Granger. "What the fuck are you talking about?"

Cody's expression hardens. "I'd watch what you say. Spreading rumors like that isn't going to win you any friends."

"The mayor is the only one who can fire me, so Timmons can go fuck himself. Everyone knows he's off screwing someone different every week." With that, Granger Ryan turns away to go deliver his report to the man, and I'm left with more questions than I have answers.

"Who the hell would do this?" I ask Cody. "You're the cop. You gotta have some kind of lead."

"You know I can't give you details about an ongoing investigation."

"Now that I'm part of the investigation, I've got a vested interest in you coming up with something right the fuck now."

He gives me a hard look. "I'm working on it. I've got leads. I'm hoping to have answers soon."

A car door slams, and we watch Memphis Lockwood and her cameraman drive away from the Four Corners in the direction of the Sleep Over.

"If you don't, my money says she will."

My phone rings as I pull the Olds 442 into my driveway an hour later. Banner looks over at me when I pull it out of my pocket.

"Boone Thrasher."

"I bet he's heard." She reaches for the door handle. "I'll get out of your way. I need a shower."

"I'll meet you inside."

I answer the phone. "Hey, Thrasher."

"Tell me that my car didn't go up in flames, man. One of the roadies sent me the link to a story that your shop blew up tonight. What the fuck?"

"I'm sitting in it right now. She's fine, not a scratch on her."

"How the fuck is that possible?"

"By the grace of God, I guess."

I fill Boone in on what happened and what I know, which isn't much, but he's relieved all the same.

"The cops going to hassle you for leaving to bring the car? I can't come get it, and honestly, I don't fucking trust anyone enough to take my truck and get it. The only other guy who drove my last one rolled it. Big mess."

"It won't be a problem. Your car will be there tomorrow. The cops won't keep me from delivering it."

"Only if you're sure, man. This shit is unbelievable."

"You're telling me."

"Well, I appreciate that my ride is safe and no one was hurt."

"Me too, man. Me too."

We hang up, and I climb out of the car and head into the house. I hear the sound of the shower as I make my way down the hall toward the bedroom.

What a fucking nightmare. This town is falling apart, and now the only thing that was keeping me locked down in Gold Haven is a pile of charred rubble.

I've got a whole lot of decisions to make now.

I step into the bathroom to see Banner naked in the shower. I've lost count of how many times I've thanked every force above that she was clear of the shop when it blew. A few minutes later and she might have been right in the blast zone.

She turns and wipes away the fog from the glass so she can meet my gaze. Her reddened eyes and tearstained face twist my gut. I hate seeing her cry.

But she isn't focused on herself. Even now, she's focused on me and my problems.

"Everything okay with Boone?"

I nod. "Yeah. He heard the news. Wanted to make sure the car was okay."

"Screw the car." She sniffles. "I know I'm not supposed to say that, but . . ." Her face turns into a mask of pain as her eyes fill with tears again. "I thought I was going to die right along with you."

I strip off my clothes, needing her in my arms. Needing to make her feel safe again. I pull open the door, step into the shower, and wrap my arms around her.

"I got you, baby. I'm right here. There's no way I'm leaving this Earth when I've got you here waiting for me."

"You can't promise that. Bad things happen."

"I can promise I'll do everything in my power to make sure I end every night with you by my side."

She hiccups, pressing her forehead to my chest. "I really fucking love you, Logan. Don't ever scare me like that again."

"I really fucking love you too, Banner Regent."

She releases a long breath, and I squeeze her tighter.

My thoughts from earlier come back. The rest of my life might be falling to shit, but with her in my arms, I've got everything that matters.

Banner lifts her head and wraps her arms around my neck, pulling my lips down to hers. "I need you. I need to feel you. To know this is real. Please."

"You don't even have to ask."

I pour everything I have into our kiss, and only when Banner is writhing against me do I push inside her.

She's right. We both need this. I lift her up and press her against the wall, fucking into her over and over while I whisper her name like a prayer.

I drop my head against the wall of the shower as we come together.

She's my everything. I will not lose her.

THIRTY-SIX

Banner

THE NEXT DAY, WE'RE TWO HOURS LATE LEAVING Gold Haven with Boone Thrasher's car in a trailer towed behind Logan's truck. By some miracle, Logan's truck didn't even have a bubble on the paint, even though it was only twenty feet away from the blaze. Something about wind direction and hand-of-God type stuff.

Logan dealt with insurance people all morning before he could finally get away and load up the car with Jock and Rick's help. Both of them swore on the graves of their respective ancestors that neither was making meth in the bathroom, and Logan believes them.

They've both been questioned by Cody Reeves too, so now all that's left is to figure out who would set up Logan like this.

He isn't the kind of guy who goes around racking up enemies. He's a good guy. The kind who doesn't hesitate to help his neighbors or do a favor for a friend.

I saw Julianne this morning, standing out in front of

her salon and directing the glass people as they measured for a new window. Her expression was hard.

"This shit is personal now. I'm gonna figure it out if the cops and that reporter can't."

From the determination in her tone, I believe she will. I just hope someone does before there are any more "accidents."

The entire town seems to be walking on eggshells, and it makes me wonder what Gold Haven was like before all of its residents looked at each other with suspicion in their eyes.

I ask Logan the question, and he spends an hour telling me stories about different people in town and how it used to be.

"Do you think things will ever go back to normal?" I ask.

In the driver's seat, his posture stiffens. "I sure as fuck hope so. But now I've got decisions to make."

"What do you mean?"

"The insurance money will let me rebuild somewhere else if I want. It won't be as much as if I rebuild the structure that was lost, but now's my chance to leave Gold Haven, if that's what I wanted to do."

"You want to leave Gold Haven?"

He glances over at me. "The town hasn't been all that welcoming to you, and that alone makes me think about it."

I'm touched that he's even considering it, but I hate the idea of being the reason he leaves his home.

"But it's your town. Where else would you go?"

Logan shrugs. "I could start over. Maybe Nashville. I hear some people really like it there. You'd have an actual city. Starbucks and all that shit you're missing."

I raise a hand. "Whoa. Just hold on. If I wanted a Starbucks on every corner, I could go back to New York to get my fix."

Logan's expression blanks. "You want to go back to New York?"

"I want to be where you are, Logan. But I don't want you deciding to move your entire life because you think it's something I want. Sure, some of the women in Gold Haven could win awards for epic bitches of the century, but I've handled most of them. I mean, I'm going to have the whole retiree contingent wanting to be my best friend because I've got the good dick." I wink at him. "Besides, I'm not going to let the Tricias or Emmys of this town run me out. I've got pride too, you know."

"So, what are you saying? You'd be happy to stay there? Run your business there?"

"Not for every day of the year. I know with your business there it would be our home base, but I'd like to spend a little time in New York, maybe travel some too. But ultimately, I've gotten used to the idea of living there. I like your house. I like going to Pints and Pins, although I might need to take some street-fighter lessons before we go back again. Unless you really want to leave, I say we stay."

Logan is quiet for a few miles before he finally answers. "Then we stay. I'll rebuild. You need an office that's not a kitchen counter, so that means we add on to the house, or you can rent space somewhere else if you don't want to work at home."

"Okay. Let me give it some thought, and I'll get back to you on that." I reach across the center console and squeeze his hand.

Everything is going to work out.

I hope.

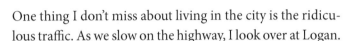

One thing I don't miss about living in the city is the ridiculous traffic. As we slow on the highway, I look over at Logan.

"I'm so sorry I didn't realize how big of a pain in the ass it would be to maneuver this big-ass trailer through Manhattan."

He shoots me a smile. "It was worth it, babe. More than worth it."

"I'm glad you feel that way, because I would've wanted to strangle me for being so clueless."

Nashville traffic slows to a crawl as we get closer and closer to downtown and the arena.

"Are you sure we're going to be able to get in there?"

"Boone says he told them we were coming."

As if the man knew we were talking about him, Logan's phone dings from the cupholder with a text.

"Wanna check that?"

I grab it and read the text, then send Logan's reply.

BOONE: *Security says they haven't seen you yet.*
LOGAN: *Almost there. GPS says 10 minutes.*
BOONE: *Good. Everyone's waiting.*

"Nothing like a little pressure," Logan mumbles as he signals to change lanes for our exit.

"It's all good, babe. He's going to love the car, and you're going to have more business than you can handle."

"Which is great, when I don't have a shop."

It's something I've been thinking about since he brought it up earlier. "I did some googling while we stopped for gas, and there's commercial space available in Gold Haven. I found you two buildings I think could work. You'd have to move the new equipment you buy back to your permanent location after you rebuild, but it would be good for now."

Logan changes lanes and glances at me. "Seriously?"

"What can I say? I wanted to help."

"Thank you, babe." He reaches over and squeezes my thigh with a smile before making the next turn.

Finally, the arena comes into view. We're only five minutes behind schedule, so I count that as a win.

When we turn around the back side of the building, two huge tour buses are parked inside a fenced area. Security stands in front of the gate.

Logan stops before opening his window. "Logan Brantley for Boone Thrasher."

"We've been waiting for you." The security guard pulls a pass out of his back pocket. "Hang this from your mirror so it's visible at all times. Pull right through here and park off to the left next to the buses."

He steps back and waves for someone else to open the gate. People are milling around outside the fence, and security keeps them from running inside the fenced-off area.

Crazy fans, I guess.

"Can't believe this is finally happening," Logan says.

I reach over and lay a hand on his arm. "You should be proud. You rocked this, babe."

He meets my gaze before pulling forward. "You know, I am. I don't think I've felt this proud since before I took off my uniform for the last time."

"Did you happen to keep that uniform? I mean, I'm just asking because . . ." I shoot him a wicked smile. "I like the idea of role-playing with my soldier."

He gives me a sharp look. "Marine, and don't you forget it."

I salute him. "Got it."

Logan pulls up next to a fancy tour bus and parks. We both climb out of the cab of the truck, and a man in ripped jeans, a black T-shirt, boots, and a shredded baseball hat comes toward us.

"I haven't been this excited since I was sure my folks got me a Red Ryder BB gun for Christmas. I'm dying to see her." He pauses and looks to me. "I'm Boone Thrasher."

"Banner Regent. Nice to meet you. You're going to love the car."

"I know. Let's get her out."

Logan smiles as we walk around the back of the trailer and unlock the doors. A few more people dressed all in black, who I assume are roadies, join the group around the trailer.

The rear end of the red-and-black car gleams in the sunlight.

"Holy fuck."

"Wait until you see the rest of her." Logan hauls out the little ramp things that will be used to drive the car out of the trailer.

"I can't wait."

Logan fishes the keys out of his pocket. "You want me to back it out?"

Boone shakes his head. "No, I got it. I've done this a

time or two."

"You screw it up, that's on you."

I'm honestly shocked at how blunt Logan is with him, but then again, I can't blame him either.

"Ten-four, brother. No worries."

Boone jumps up into the back of the trailer, swearing as he runs his hand along the paint job. When the ramps are in place, Logan yells to him to fire it up.

The engine roars to life, and over the sound, I can hear Boone laughing. Everyone holds their breath as he backs it out of the trailer and down the ramps.

I've been so busy watching what was happening in front of me, I didn't realize all the press crowding around us until the click of camera shutters catches my attention.

Now it makes sense why Boone wanted to be the one to back it out. He may look like a simple country guy, but he's savvy with the press.

When the Olds 442 is parked on solid ground, Logan finally breathes again.

Boone revs the engine, laughing like a crazy person. "This is so fucking badass!"

When he finally turns the engine off, opens the door and climbs out, he throws both arms around Logan. "Amazing, man. You killed it. The shifter knob with my logo. The paint. The interior. It's just like you drew it. I can't even fucking believe it."

"Glad you like her. She's a beauty."

"She's a snarlin' beast and the baddest bitch to ever roll off a trailer. I can't wait to get her onstage. This show is gonna be epic. The car, the new single, and my surprise."

I don't know what surprise Boone's talking about, but

apparently he doesn't want the press to know about it either because he doesn't elaborate.

"You wanna see under the hood?" Logan asks.

"Hell yeah." Boone crouches near the door and reaches inside for the hood release. Logan comes around the front and props it open.

"Holy shit. Look at that setup."

I don't know anything about anything when it comes to cars, but even I think all the shiny metal looks impressive.

Logan runs down the entire list of *what makes this car badass*, but it all goes right over my head. Apparently Boone doesn't have that problem, because he's nodding and grinning.

"It's gonna take all the restraint I've got not to take her to the track and race for pinks like I used to."

Logan gives him a hard look. "If you're gonna take that chance, I want first dibs."

Boone holds out his hand. "Thank you, man. This is truly a masterpiece."

The press has been hanging back, snapping pictures, but when Boone waves them forward, I'm instantly behind a crowd of people.

As Logan answers questions, his commanding confidence is sexy as hell. I cross my arms, content to watch him in his element.

The press has already heard about the destruction of the shop, and when they ask, Logan handles it like a pro.

"Despite the devastating loss, I'm already making plans to rebuild. I think from Boone's reaction, it's clear that I need to get my new temporary location up and running as quickly as possible. We'll be able to handle all projects coming our way."

"So, does Boone get to keep you with the car?"

Someone with a drawl more pronounced than Logan's steps up beside me. I look to the right and see a guy in a worn gray thermal, ripped jeans, and boots.

His question catches me off guard. "Uh, no."

The man gives me a head-to-toe look, lingering on the predictable spots. "Might be better for him if he could. But then again, since he's a *committed man*," he throws up air quotes around the last two words, "you'd just end up going home with me anyway."

"I'm not sure who you think you are, but—"

He holds out a big hand. "Nashville recording artist Zane Frisco at your service, beautiful. And when I say at your service, I do mean it. You tell me when and where." When I don't reply, he asks, "And you are?"

"Not interested."

His eyes widen just enough to let me know that's not the usual reaction he gets. "Honey, you don't realize who you're talking to, do you?"

I straighten my shoulders and turn to face him. "It doesn't really matter. You know why?" I point at Logan. "You see that guy? The one who built this badass car? He's mine and I'm his. So all the flirting in the world isn't going to be anything but a waste of your breath. I'm taken. Off the market. Well and truly not interested."

"When you put it like that, it just makes you even more of a challenge. That kind of loyalty is hard to come by in a woman."

I cross my arms. "That might be true, but that sounds like a *you* problem." Glancing back toward Logan, I notice his gaze is on Zane Frisco and me.

"Sure you don't want to make him jealous, beautiful?"

I look away from Logan and back to Zane. "Completely."

Something lights in his gray eyes. "Well, maybe I do." He reaches out an arm to wrap around my hips, but I spin out of his reach just as quickly.

"If you have an interest in preserving your ability to perform as anything but a soprano, I suggest you back off right now."

Logan strides toward us. "Is there a problem here?"

Boone is right behind him, and I'm painfully aware of the clicks of the camera shutters now.

"No problem at all," Zane says. "You're a lucky man. If you're a smart one too, you'll put a ring on that woman's finger so the whole world knows she's taken."

Logan's hand lands on the small of my back. "Thanks for the advice."

"Frisco, you better keep your paws off Brantley's woman. You want that rust-bucket Challenger of yours to look like my beast, this is the man who can do it."

"For double," I add with a pointed look.

Zane's deep laughter carries through the crowd. When he's finished, he reaches out his hand to Logan. "No offense meant, man. Zane Frisco. I'd be proud to have a Logan Brantley custom ride."

Logan pauses a beat before gripping his hand and shaking it. "You try to touch Banner again, and the only Logan Brantley custom ride you'll get will be to the ER."

I'm not sure if they're involved in some kind of hand-shake standoff, but they finally relax their grips when Zane replies.

"Duly noted."

Boone grins at Logan. "Thanks for not breaking his hand. He's my special guest for tonight's show, and if he can't play the guitar, he's pretty worthless."

"Wouldn't dream of it." Logan's tone is as dry as I've ever heard a drawl.

"Let me grab my assistant and send her over to you. She's got your info for the hotel and the schedule for tomorrow. Have a good time tonight, and we'll see you tomorrow for all the press shit."

"Thank you, Boone. Much appreciated." Logan nods at Zane. "Frisco."

He throws his arm around me, his hand resting on my ass as he leads me back to the truck and trailer. "Do I need to go back and kick his ass?"

I glance up into Logan's blue eyes. "Would you if I said yes?"

"Damn right."

I shake my head. "No need. I can handle myself if necessary."

Logan's gaze darkens, and it's like the alpha-male possessive instincts have been cranked up to ten. "I'll handle you and anything that comes your way."

"How about you handle me back at the hotel?"

THIRTY-SEVEN

Logan

Boone Thrasher went all out, booking us a penthouse suite that's so badass, even Banner looks impressed.

Ever since we left the arena, Zane Frisco's words have been playing on a loop in my head. *Put a ring on that woman's finger so the whole world knows she's taken.*

God knows the thought has been on my mind a lot over the last couple of days. Coming to grips with the fact that I could have lost Banner in that fire has clarified everything I want: her and forever.

I'm not a rich man, and I know she deserves more than I can spend right now, especially with a burned-down business and no income, and that just makes it eat at me more.

Maybe I can't ask the question yet, but I can worship her with my body all the same.

As soon as we walk into the bedroom, Banner goes to the floor-to-ceiling windows and stares out over the sun setting on the city below.

"So beautiful," she says.

I follow her, pushing her hair aside to press a kiss to her neck. "Very beautiful."

She turns her gaze up to mine, a smile playing at the corners of her mouth. "I was talking about the city."

"I can't say I see anything but the amazing woman in front of me."

"You're a smooth talker, Logan Brantley."

"Only with you." And it's the truth. The right woman changes everything.

"I like it when you talk dirty too," Banner says, her expression morphing into one of downright mischief. Anytime she wants to play, I'm game.

"Then you're really going to like it when I tell you I'm gonna fuck you against this window, and I don't care who sees."

Banner bites down on her lip for a beat before reaching back to skim a hand down my side. "Oh yeah? You want my palms and tits pressed to the glass as you take me from behind so they can see my face when you make me come?"

"I want them to hear you scream my name all the way down on the street."

She spins around and her hands tear at my clothes. Banner yanks my shirt over my head, and then her fingers go for the button of my jeans, shoving them down.

"Maybe they should see me on my knees first, taking your cock down my throat."

I groan as she palms my hard dick and kneels. "Fuck yes." I bury my fingers in her hair as she swipes her tongue over the head. "Mine. All fucking mine."

She looks up at me. "You mean, *mine*. I'm never letting you go, Logan Brantley."

"I wouldn't let you. I fucking love you, Banner."

Her smile widens before she takes my dick in her mouth. I keep my eyes locked on hers as she works me with her lips, tongue, and throat. I have to pull away within minutes, because there's no way in hell I'm coming down her throat.

I pull Banner to her feet and strip her bare. Her hair tumbles around her shoulders in a sexy mess.

"Turn around. We're going to show them exactly who you belong to."

She turns toward the glass, and I wrap one hand around her throat and tilt her head back until it touches my shoulder. My other hand circles her nipple, teasing and tugging until she's writhing into my palm.

"You're always so fucking responsive." I leave her tits to go lower, cupping her pussy. "This is mine."

"Only yours."

"Always."

"Yes."

I find her clit with a fingertip and circle it, bringing her to the edge of orgasm before I say the words that have been on my mind. "I'm gonna marry you, Banner. Give you my name. My kids. This is forever."

"Yes!" she yells as she comes, and I bury a finger inside her to keep her body on the edge.

When she's begging for another orgasm, I pull my fingers away and release my grip on her throat to spin her around.

"Say it again."

"Yes." Her gaze collides with mine. "Absolutely yes."

I lift her up and carry her away from the window.

"I changed my mind. This is only for us. No one else gets to see you, hear you. I'm greedy for every single piece of you, and I'll never have enough."

I lay her down on the massive bed and hold her gaze as I slide inside her.

"I love you, Logan."

"I'm going to spend the rest of my life making sure you never regret it."

But first, I spend the rest of the night making her repeat her *yes* over and over again.

This woman is mine.

Forever.

THIRTY-EIGHT

Banner

THE NEXT DAY PASSES AT LIGHTNING SPEED. THE press and all the car magazines lose their minds over Logan's custom detail work on Boone's car. I stand proudly to the side as I watch my man get the credit he deserves. At home, there's a mess waiting for us, but right now, this is all that matters.

Once the press part is over, Boone invites us to come watch his sound checks. Zane Frisco is already onstage completing his when we enter the arena.

"For an arrogant asshole, he's not a bad performer," Boone says.

"So, what does that make you?"

The voice comes from the hallway that leads to backstage. We all turn to see Holly Wix step out.

Damn, for giving birth not long ago, she looks amazing. If she wasn't my best friend's sister-in-law, I might be a tiny bit jealous when she throws her arms around Logan.

"Look at you. The pride of Gold Haven," she says.

"I think that's you, Holly."

"We can share the title," she says as she steps back, and then Boone sweeps her up in a hug.

I glance out toward the hallway to see Creighton Karas, her husband, holding a pink bundle in his arms, a possessive look on his face as he watches his wife with the other men.

"Hey, little mama. I wondered when you were going to get here. I haven't told anyone, as requested," Boone says.

"Thank you. I thought it'd be easier to get back onstage if no one had any expectations." When Boone releases Holly, she looks to me. "You must be Banner. It's so nice to finally meet you in person. Thank you so much for watching Gran's house. With the baby . . ."

"You don't need to thank me. Thank *you* for letting me crash my homeless self there. We're keeping a good eye on it, I promise."

She looks from me to Logan. "It seems like everything worked out the way it's supposed to."

Creighton steps forward. "Banner. Good to see you again, and not in the press."

His sister is my best friend, and we may have caused a little bit of a PR nightmare once upon a time. I know he secretly thinks I'm awesome, though.

"Come on, Crey. I've grown out of that. Well, mostly. There was an incident with a box of dicks in Gold Haven . . ."

Crey shakes his head. "I don't even want to know, do I?" When I just smile, his attention shifts to Logan and then back to me. "I never would've guessed backwoods rednecks were your type."

Indignation dumps into my veins. "You watch your

billionaire mouth, Creighton Karas. I don't care who your father is. I'll shove—"

Logan's arm snakes around my waist and tugs me back against him. "It's okay, Bruce. We go way back."

"All right, you two. Enough." Holly lifts the pink bundle, complete with ear protection, from Creighton's arms. "No fighting in front of Rose."

The baby's tiny nose and perfect rosebud mouth melt away all the F-bombs I planned to drop on Creighton Karas, and I remember what Logan said about kids.

I've never had that *oh my God, I want one of those* feeling before, but it slams into me. Hard.

"Can I hold her?" I'm slightly terrified I just asked, because I've never held a baby.

"Of course," Holly says. "We want her to be comfortable with all sorts of people holding her."

"Show me how?"

Holly smiles as she places her in my arms. "You're a natural."

Logan's hand presses against me tighter for a beat, and I have a feeling the man is going to try to knock me up as soon as possible. For the first time in my life, the thought doesn't terrify me.

"Damn. Pretty as a picture, Banner," Boone says before turning back to Holly. "Crey can handle the baby for a while, right? Let's run through the song while I've got you here."

"We brought the nanny too."

"I'm perfectly capable of taking care of my daughter," Creighton replies.

And true to his word, when Rose starts to fuss in my

arms, he closes the distance between us and gently takes her from me.

"Hush, sweet girl. Daddy's here. What do you need?" When she continues to fuss, he says, "Fine. You can have a pony when you're four. Not a day sooner. You have to wait for the Maserati until you're sixteen and have taken tactical driving lessons."

Holly's laugh echoes off the walls. "God help you if we have any more kids. We'll be bankrupt if you have to buy them all the stuff you've promised her."

But the baby is quiet, peacefully sleeping in her father's arms. He shoots Holly a look. "It works."

"Maybe she'll want a Mustang like her mama."

"If she's anything like her mama, I'm keeping her locked up until she's forty. Never mind, I'm doing that anyway. Let's go, sweet girl. Daddy's taking you back to the tour bus. We've got a few more chapters of *Millionaire Next Door* to pass the time while Mommy does her famous thing."

If someone had told me two years ago that I'd ever hear those words coming out of Creighton Karas's mouth, I would have thought they were drunk and popping pills.

Holly shakes her head as he walks down the hallway toward backstage and what I'm assuming is the exit to where the tour buses are parked.

"He bought a new tour bus for the sole purpose of turning half of it into a nursery. I swear, without me, that girl would be spoiled rotten."

"I think that's what you call balance."

"All right, enough baby talk. Let's go make some music magic, Wix."

Boone and Holly head for the stage, and Logan and I

stay where we are and watch. It is, indeed, magic.

We head back to the hotel an hour later so I can meet the stylist Boone's assistant is sending over to do my hair and makeup for the concert, but when we hit the lobby, Logan tells me to go ahead by myself because he forgot something he had to take care of.

"If I don't make it back in time, have the driver take you to the venue, and I'll meet you there."

I don't argue because I know he wants everything to be perfect with the car for Boone's show. "Go. Do what you need to do."

He kisses me hard before turning and striding away.

I'm not going to lie and say I don't watch his perfect ass in those jeans until he disappears from sight.

BANNER: *Heading to the stadium now. You there already?*
MY SEXY MAN: *I'll be there soon.*

I glance up at the driver through the partition and wonder where the hell Logan is if he's not at the venue. I figured he was already there working on the car, but maybe I missed him? Who knows.

When the car slows and security waves us through the same back gate Logan and I used yesterday, I tuck my phone back in my purse.

My hair and makeup are perfection, and I'm in love with the silver flowy top, designer jean miniskirt, and handmade dress boots the stylist brought for me as well. I look the part for a country concert.

With my all-access pass around my neck, I head toward

the door I left from earlier today, and security waves me through. Boone's assistant is waiting inside.

"Where's Logan? Is he behind you?"

"I thought he was already here, but I guess he's on his way."

She looks marginally annoyed, probably because we've created more work for her, but she hides it well. "If you come with me, there's a VIP room where you can help yourself to dinner and drinks. I'll take you to the spot where you can stand and watch the show before Zane goes on."

I mill around the room where she leaves me, deciding to wait and eat when Logan arrives, but I order a vodka tonic at the bar.

Zane Frisco steps up beside me. "Bourbon. Whatever you've got that's not shit," he says to the bartender before looking over at me as I squeeze my lemon into my drink.

"I'm surprised your man let you out alone in that."

"He's on his way. And we've already covered the fact that he's got nothing to worry about."

"So, how does a classy piece like you end up with a mechanic from Kentucky?"

I raise an eyebrow. "Someone's been stalking. You got a crush on Logan now?"

"I'm deciding if I'm going to let him touch my Challenger."

"You'd be an idiot not to. He's damn good." I keep the fact that his shop is now mostly rubble to myself. If Zane doesn't already know, it's not my job to fill him in.

A redhead whose nipples are barely covered by her tiny white tank top interrupts us by holding up a Sharpie. "Zane, do you mind signing my shirt?" It reads Frisky for

FRISCO across the chest.

Zane takes the marker from her. "I'd be happy to. What's your name, darlin'?"

I take that as my chance to escape and head across the room where Creighton Karas is walking in, baby carrier strapped to his chest over his custom-tailored shirt. The back of the black baby carrier reads MOMMY's #1 FAN in pink glittery script.

"Jesus Christ, Crey. Who knew you'd be so domesticated or that a guy with a baby could be so hot?"

"Sounds like you're heading toward domestication yourself. Greer filled me in this afternoon when we talked. You're planning on making the move to Kentucky permanent?"

I nod. "I am."

"Impressive change of pace."

"Sometimes that's good."

"You don't have to justify it to me. I have a soft spot for that town, if only because it produced the most incredible woman I've ever met." His expression sobers. "But I hear there's been some . . . less-than-positive things happening there lately."

I'm not sure if he chooses the oblique way of describing the meth epidemic because of the people hanging around or because of the baby sleeping with her head pressed against him.

"You could say that."

"What can I do to help?"

In hushed tones, I tell him about the reporter, the police chief, the meth houses, and finally Logan's shop.

"The reporter and cops have no leads?"

I tip my drink back. "I don't know. It doesn't seem like it."

"I can send a team down there to start investigating. I've got a vested interest in that town getting back to normal."

"We might need it."

"You need a construction crew to rebuild? I can send two. They'll have Logan up and running in no time."

His generosity stuns me. "Are you serious?"

"It won't be free, but I won't gouge him for the rush."

"Why?"

Creighton gives a slightly bored shrug. "Because I can. And maybe because Logan Brantley helped me realize what was really important in my life." He cradles Rose's head, his thumb sweeping back and forth across her downy hair.

"I'll let him know when he gets here."

"That would be now."

I turn to follow Creighton's gaze and see Logan coming toward me. He's wearing a black pearl-snap shirt, perfectly worn jeans, black-and-brown cowboy boots, and a Boone Thrasher ball cap with brass knuckles on the front.

Holy. Hell. I want to climb him. Screw the audience.

He stops beside me and leans down to press a quick kiss to my lips. "Sorry I'm late. I had something I had to do."

"Come find me later, Brantley. We're going to talk about how fast we can get that shop of yours in business again." Creighton turns and strides away before Logan can reply.

Logan looks back to me. "Is he serious?"

I nod. "I think he feels like he owes you for something. And here's the only advice I'm going to give on the subject. When Creighton Karas offers you his help, take it. Especially this time. He might seem like an arrogant jackhole, because

227

he is, but he can also be a pretty decent human being."

Logan considers me thoughtfully. "I'll talk to him." His arm comes around me. "But first, I want to talk to you." He pulls me away from the crowd and down a hallway.

"Where are we going?"

"You'll see."

He leads me into a room where the Olds 442 is waiting for Boone to drive it onstage.

"You need to say good-bye to the car?"

Logan shakes his head. "No. I've already done that. She served her purpose, and now she's his to enjoy."

"So, what are we doing? Oh shit, you want to break it in one more time? Backstage?"

He shakes his head again. "No. I have to say something."

His serious tone puts me on edge.

"What's going on?" Something about Logan seems off, making my nerves ping.

"I would've picked somewhere fancier for this, but that's not my speed. I'm just a guy who works with his hands and happens to have a knack for restoring cars."

"You're more than that," I say, but he holds up a hand so I go silent, wondering what he's leading up to. My heart rate kicks up a notch in nervous anticipation.

"I was sitting in this car when I realized that if I don't have you in my life, I don't have anything, Banner. Everything else I want means nothing if I don't have you to share it with."

He pulls something out of his pocket and drops to one knee.

Oh my God. Tears spring to my eyes as he takes my hand and holds up a small silver band with . . . the X-Men symbol on it.

"I can't buy you the big diamond ring you deserve right now, but someday I will."

A tear slides down my cheek.

"I love you, Banner Regent, and I want you to be my wife. Marry me."

Another tear falls as I nod and drop to my knees in front of him. "I don't want a big diamond ring. I just want you."

Logan slides the X-Men ring on my finger. "Good, because that's all I've got to offer."

He cups my face and covers my lips with his. I don't know how long we stay locked together, but someone eventually clears their throat from behind us.

"Uh . . . sorry to interrupt, but the opening act goes on in ten. We gotta—"

Logan rises and lifts me to my feet before swinging me up into his arms. "We'll get out of your way."

He carries me back down the hallway, and we run into Boone as he opens the door to his dressing room.

"Well, fuck. You just had to beat me to it, didn't ya?"

How does he know? I follow his gaze to my left hand. *Well, I guess the ring does give it away.*

"Not trying to upstage you, but I'm not apologizing either."

When Logan lowers me to my feet, Boone slaps him on the shoulder. "Congratulations, you two." He reaches into his pocket and pulls out an enormous diamond solitaire. "I've never been so damned nervous in my life. Never thought I would be. This next flight better not be late. That's all I can say. She was supposed to be here three hours ago,

MEGHAN MARCH

but she missed the earlier one."

"Good luck," I say, leaning into Logan.

Boone nods and closes the door to his dressing room.

Logan looks down at my ring finger. "I swear, I'm going to get you—"

I lift my hand and press two fingers to Logan's lips. "No. This is us, Logan. And it's perfect."

He moves my finger and rubs his thumb over the X. "I had to play eighteen games of hoops at the arcade to win enough tickets for this bad boy. And it took me three arcades to find the right prize to begin with."

"That's why you're late?" Laughter bubbles up in my throat.

"Damn right."

I wrap both arms around his neck and kiss the hell out of my future husband.

THIRTY-NINE

Logan

HOLLY AND BOONE KILL IT WITH THEIR DUET, BUT Boone looks more stressed than ever. From the tizzy his assistant is in, it's pretty obvious his girlfriend is still a no-show. I feel for the guy, even as I watch with pride as he drives the rumbling Olds 442 onstage, climbs out, and tells the entire crowd the story behind the car.

"Even when she was more rust than metal, I knew she was a diamond in the rough. So I wrote a song, my newest single, and I'm going to debut it here tonight for you."

The crowd screams in excitement, and he waits for them to quiet down before nodding to the drummer, who counts off the beat.

Boone's gravelly voice fills the massive space.

I'm gonna take a ride with you
In my 442.
Rolling down the same old roads
Like we always do.
Other things may change,

My love remains the same.
With you by my side
In my new old ride,
In my 442.

He keeps looking toward where we stand as if hoping his girlfriend is going to show, but she doesn't. When he finishes the song, he tells the crowd good night and God bless before striding offstage without playing an encore.

Banner and I exchange looks.

"That's not good."

"Poor guy."

"I'm sure he'll figure something out."

But I've got way more important things on my mind than Boone's woman. "Now, we celebrate."

Banner's eyes light with excitement. "What do you have planned?"

"What do you think?"

She glances down at her ring. "It's my turn to win you a ring, isn't it?"

"If you're game." I pull Banner into my arms.

She presses a kiss to my neck. "I'm game for anything with you."

"That's my girl."

"Even if it's a cock ring?" she asks, one eyebrow raised.

My laugh booms between us. "I guess we'll see about that."

FORTY

Logan

I TURNED MY PHONE OFF ON SATURDAY NIGHT AS SOON as I got to the stadium, so when I turn it back on to check the GPS for the quickest route out of Nashville on Sunday morning, I'm not surprised when a few texts show up.

CODY: *Need you at the station Monday morning to answer questions. Better be there.*

GRANGER: *State investigator and I both think the fire was arson. Not meth. Official report won't be out until next week, but shit looks bad.*

JULIANNE: *I need to talk to you. Call me as soon as you get this.*

"What do you think Julianne wants?" Banner asks.

"Don't know, but I'll call her to find out when we get closer."

"Don't you think you should call her now?"

I squeeze her hand where it rests on the center console.

"I'd prefer to keep reality at bay for a little bit longer, if you know what I mean."

"I know, babe. But maybe she knows something. If someone deliberately set that fire . . . that's terrifying. Someone could've been killed."

I know Banner's right, but I hold off for a few more miles before grabbing my phone and calling Julianne.

She doesn't answer, so I shove the phone back in the cupholder and crank up the music.

"We're setting a date before we get out of this truck," I say as I take the exit toward Gold Haven a few hours later.

Banner looks over at me. "What?"

"You heard me. I don't want to wait too long. Seeing you hold Holly's little girl . . . Hell, Banner. That did something to me."

She laughs. "If you'd said that to me six months ago, I would've run. But now, I'm pretty okay with it."

My phone rings before I can reply. *Julianne.*

"Hello?"

When no one answers on the other end, I hit SPEAKER.

"Hello?"

"Logan?"

"Yeah."

"I think we're getting answers today. Where are you?"

Banner's gaze clashes with mine.

"Fifteen minutes outside of town. What the hell are you talking about?"

"I'm following Memphis Lockwood down County Road 45. She just left Home Cookin' like a bat out of hell while I was getting coffee, so I did too."

"Julianne, back off. Call Cody. Let him handle it."

"Can't. He's trying to find Chief Timmons. He's missing."

"What the fuck?"

"That hypocrite Timmons hasn't missed a Sunday service in twelve years since he came to town, but he missed today."

"He could be sick. Hung over. Whatever. That doesn't mean shit."

"At Home Cookin', they said no one has seen him since last night. Cody couldn't reach him, and he's not at home."

"Where are you exactly?"

"About to cross Orchard Road."

"Toward the Harris property?" I ask, picturing where she is.

"And Nicole's place."

"It ain't her."

"I guess we'll find out. Shit, the reporter just turned off onto the Harrises' land. Gotta go. Get here."

When she hangs up, Banner looks at me. "You have to explain."

"The Harrises have a compound out on County Road 45. Main house, guest house, and a couple cabins. Emmy used to live in the guest house before she built her own place on the other side of the property. Nicole rents one of the cabins from them cheap so she can save to buy the bowling alley."

"So that means . . . what?"

I shake my head. "I don't fucking know."

I haul ass there, and I'm probably ten minutes behind Julianne and the reporter when I pull onto the property. The main drive splits in two directions, right to the main house and guest house, and left to the cabins.

Even though I hate that my gut tells me to go left, I do it anyway.

When I see two cars pulled off the side of the road, I feel like I swallowed a rock. "Fuck. It can't be Nicole. No fucking way."

I park behind Julianne's Jeep, wishing she would have kept her nose out of this. The other car belongs to Memphis Lockwood and her cameraman.

"Stay here," I tell Banner.

"No fucking way. I'm going with you."

"Not a chance in hell when I don't know what I'm walking into. Stay. Here."

"Fine. But if something happens to you, I'll kick your ass myself."

I lean over the console and press a hard kiss to her lips before pulling back. "Don't worry. I'm marrying you, so I'm sure as fuck coming back in one piece. Pick a goddamned date, Banner."

I reach beneath the seat, pull out my gun, and climb out of the truck.

FORTY-ONE

Logan

I TUCK MY 9MM INTO THE BACK OF MY JEANS AND STAY in the cover of brush as I make my way up to the cabin. It's times like this when all of Uncle Sam's training comes right back like I never took my camis off.

The yelling reaches me first. A man. No, two men. And at least two women. It's coming from Nicole's cabin.

The small wooden structure has a front door and a back door. It's mostly two big rooms—a living room and kitchen, and the bedroom. The bathroom is walled off most of the way to the ceiling, but open above. There's a tiny kitchenette along the east wall, and that's where I head because of the little window above the sink.

The glass looks like it hasn't been washed in an age, but through the film, I can make out a few people.

What in the ever-loving fuck?

Police Chief Timmons is facedown on the floor in the living room, and there's a dark puddle around his head. *Jesus fucking Christ.* If he's alive, it'll be a miracle.

Memphis Lockwood is nowhere in sight, but I can hear

Julianne's muffled voice inside the cabin. The man inside turns to the left, and I get a better look.

Rusty Mills? I haven't seen him since the bowling alley incident with Emmy, the night Banner got punched in the face by Tricia. Rusty has Nicole tied to a chair, and fury burns through me when he swings and connects with her face. Her head lolls to the side before falling limp.

He's a dead man.

I reach for my phone, but it's not in my pocket. *Shit, I left it in the truck.*

Banner's smart, though, which means I sure as hell hope she's calling Cody.

A stick cracks, and I yank my gun out of my jeans and whip around to find Memphis Lockwood behind me.

She raises her hands. "Don't shoot me. Please. I'm just trying to get the truth."

"Jesus fucking Christ, woman. Watch your step. You call the cops?"

"Service sucks out here, but I think they're coming. God, I hope so."

"What the hell happened?" I ask, keeping my voice low and staying out of sight.

"I hid in the woods when I heard someone coming behind me. I thought maybe it was the property owner, but it was the hairdresser. She tried to look in the windows, but the man saw her and dragged her inside. I was more careful. I think Timmons is dead, though."

I'm still processing everything she said and working out a plan of attack when Memphis's eyes go wide at the unmistakable sound of a revolver being cocked behind me.

"Put the gun on the ground, and turn around."

I turn and face Emmy Harris. "What the hell are you doing, Emmy?"

"You're trespassing." She swings the barrel from me to Memphis and back again.

The sight before me doesn't make any sense. "Did you call the cops, Emmy? Rusty has Julianne, Nicole, and Timmons inside."

Her mouth drops open into a little O. "You don't say?"

A shot is fired in the cabin, and Julianne's muffled voice goes quiet.

Instead of fear, the only feeling inside me is the familiar coldness I honed as a marine.

Emmy smiles, but it's not a smile like I've ever seen before. "Who do you think he shot?" She blinks, and the smile dies. "You're gonna be next, Logan, if you don't put that gun on the ground like I said."

One thing you learn real fast in battle is that not having a gun means you're dead.

Emmy swings the gun back to Memphis. "You have three seconds before I shoot her, and it'll be all your fault that she dies. At this range, there's no way I can miss."

Knowing she was captain of the girl's trap-shooting team in high school, I don't doubt her aim for a second. And nothing except the loss of someone else's life could convince me to put my gun down.

I crouch and lay it in the leaves at my feet.

"Do I look like an idiot? Kick it toward me."

I follow her directions, but start talking. "Whatever Rusty made you do, you can tell Cody and Timmons, and I'm sure they'll understand it was all under duress."

Emmy laughs. "Timmons is already dead. And now

you're all gonna join him because I'm not going down for this. Can you imagine what my parents would say?"

"Why'd you do it, Emmy?" This question comes from Memphis. "The meth? I know you've been using your supplier's trucks to ship it out of town, and you planted it in Logan's shop and set the explosion as a distraction."

Emmy narrows her eyes on Memphis, making me wish the woman would shut up, because the look on Emmy's face says her patience is gone.

"You think you're so smart, don't you? Big-city reporter, coming down here and getting into things that are none of your business. What makes you think I have anything to do with it?"

Memphis, who I have to admit has a pair of brass balls, sounds bored as she replies. "I followed the money. And you've been hemorrhaging it for over a year. Your CPA sold you out, Emmy. Don't ever stop paying your accountant. They know all the dirty secrets. What are your parents going to think when they find out you spent every dollar the restaurant made and more? It's embezzlement when you don't own it."

"Fucking Ashcroft. He'll pay. I've got more dirt on him than he'll survive." Emmy's tone drips acid as she talks about the CPA.

The door to the cabin slams, and Rusty comes around the side of the building, gun in hand.

"Ain't this quite the little party. Too bad they'll never find your bodies."

"Whose idea was it?" Memphis asks, apparently not able to resist her reporter's nature.

"The meth?" Rusty shrugs. "Mine. And since Emmy

didn't have a problem keeping Timmons too busy fucking her tight little cunt to investigate a damn thing, we could've kept this going forever." He shakes his head. "But no. Y'all had to get nosy."

The pieces fall together.

"You stole from your family and sold meth to make the money back." My tone is low, but Emmy's attention swings back to me.

"I knew you were more than just a pretty face and a hard body, Logan. It's too bad you didn't fall in line. I really would've liked to marry you. I wouldn't have spent nearly so much money on that house if I hadn't been making it perfect for us."

"The hell you say," Rusty interjects. "You said you were over him. That house was gonna be for you and me. You're just a cheating bitch like the rest of them, aren't you? I bet you liked fucking Timmons too."

Rusty raises his gun at Emmy, but Emmy's quicker on the trigger. The percussion from the shot is deafening at close range.

I grab Memphis's arm and drag her to the ground before diving for my gun. But Emmy has already turned, and the barrel of her revolver presses against my forehead as my hand reaches metal.

"No one calls me a bitch," Emmy says, her tone conversational. "Especially not Rusty Mills."

"Oh really, because I have no fucking problem calling you a bitch."

Something inside me dies when I hear Banner's voice ring out from beyond the cabin, and the barrel lifts from my head as Emmy turns toward her.

No fucking way am I going to lose her now.

"You're like a bad case of the clap, city girl. Just showing up when you least expect it and completely unwelcome," Emmy says. "But thankfully, I know how to get rid of both."

I close my hand around the grip of my gun and launch myself at Emmy from behind, yanking her feet out from under her. Her shot goes wild, and someone screams.

Fear that rivals what I felt when I drove up on my shop in flames tears through me faster than the shot. I pounce on top of Emmy, my 9mm inches from her face.

"Banner!"

"The bitch shot me!"

My Glock has no safety, and the only thing stopping me from pulling the trigger is the sound of Banner's voice.

"Where? Memphis, get to her!"

As Memphis rushes toward Banner, I wrap a hand around Emmy's wrist and flip her over, wishing I had a zip tie or a rope, anything to tie her up with. But I don't, so I crush her wrists together with a near bone-breaking grip.

"You're hurting me."

"Banner! Answer me!"

"I'm okay. I think. Mostly."

Banner's voice comes closer and I look up. Memphis is walking with an arm around her, and blood drips from the upper edge of Banner's arm.

"Grazed her."

"Crazy bitch!" This comes from Julianne as she stumbles down the cabin stairs, the door slamming shut behind her. "You could've killed her! You killed him!"

"Everyone, put your fucking guns down. Hands up. Right now," Cody yells from the path leading to the cabin.

I lower my pistol and raise the other hand. "Emmy tried to kill all of us. She killed Rusty. Maybe Timmons too."

"What the fuck? Someone needs to explain what the hell happened. Now."

FORTY-TWO

Banner

CODY PUTS A HAND ON EMMY'S HEAD AND SHOVES her into the back of his cruiser. The coroner pronounced Police Chief Timmons and Rusty dead on the scene—Timmons from blunt force trauma to the head, and Rusty from the gunshot wound to the chest. Cody called the county forensics unit to investigate because the whole scene was a clusterfuck.

Emmy started singing immediately, telling Cody she and Rusty showed up at Nicole's cabin to find out what Nicole told the police, and then they lured Timmons by making Nicole tell him she'd sleep with him if he'd look for information elsewhere and leave her alone.

Nicole told Cody they tried to pay her to kill him, and she pretended to go along with the plan until Timmons showed up and she outed them on purpose. Rusty bashed Timmons in the head and tied him up, but he died from the injury before they could decide what to do with him.

Rusty beat the hell out of Nicole and shot Julianne in the shoulder. EMTs swept them off to the hospital in an ambulance, but I refused to go until Cody understood that Logan had done nothing wrong.

Memphis took notes through the whole thing, and called her cameraman immediately. As soon as they finished filming, she left in a hurry to edit the piece and get it back to her network.

Luckily, Emmy barely winged me, and the paramedics cleaned the wound and slapped a few butterfly bandages on it since I wouldn't leave the scene. The bitch did ruin my shirt, though.

As soon as I heard that first gunshot, I called Cody from Logan's phone. He told me to do the same thing Logan did—stay put.

But I've never been really good at following directions.

Apparently Emmy had overspent on building her little house, and started "borrowing" money from the restaurant until it was running in the red. Rusty had done a few odd jobs for her and found out about her money problems, and told her he knew a good way to make them go away.

Once she put the cash back, she couldn't stop. I think the country saying is *pigs get fat, hogs get slaughtered*. In this case, Emmy and Rusty were both hogs.

If I hadn't seen it happen and heard it myself, I wouldn't believe it either.

Cody slams the door of the police cruiser and says something to Logan. After the men shake hands, Logan strides toward me, anger etched into his every feature.

"I told you to stay—"

"Wednesday. This Wednesday."

He stops in front of me. "What the hell are you talking about?"

"You told me not to get out of the truck until I picked a date. I picked Wednesday," I tell him.

Logan closes his eyes for a moment, and I'm pretty sure he's praying for patience.

"Don't you ever put yourself in that kind of danger again."

I drop a hand onto my hip. "I could say the same thing to you. What the hell would I do without a real man to keep me in line? My vibrators might be amazeballs, but they're no substitute for you."

Logan yanks me into his arms and buries his face in my hair. My shoulder twinges where the bullet winged me, and I stiffen.

Logan drops his arms. "Fuck. I'm sorry, baby. You sure you don't need the hospital?"

"I'm sure. Let's go home."

He wraps an arm around me and leads me toward the truck. "I will turn your ass red if you ever do anything like that again."

A smile tugs at the corners of my mouth. "You promise?"

EPILOGUE

Logan

One year later

VIBRATORS RACE ACROSS THE BAR, ONE PINK AND one blue.

Banner bounces as much as her belly will let her when the pink one wins. "I told you she's a girl!"

Julianne shakes her head. "I demand a rematch. I swear, you're carrying a boy."

The other women chime in with their opinions, including Holly and Greer and Sofia, Banner's friend from New York, with her weird little dog, Jordana.

Nicole went all out for Banner's baby shower. Pints and Pins, which she bought from Ben with a loan from my wife, is decorated with pink-and-blue streamers. Of course they're not playing normal baby-shower games because that would be way too boring for my wife.

And yes, even eleven months and twenty-five days later, I still love saying *my wife*.

The only person of note who's missing is Banner's mom. She apparently had some kind of important experiment running and couldn't be bothered to attend her only daughter's baby shower. Not that Banner's parents came to the wedding either, which ended up happening on Friday and not Wednesday after the cabin shootout. We've invited them down for the baby's birth, but I'm not holding my breath there.

Emmy is currently incarcerated in a women's prison after taking a plea bargain and providing information to end most of the meth trade in Gold Haven. They expect she'll serve about fifteen years before getting out.

My shop, which she admitted to burning down out of spite, was up and running faster than I would have thought possible, courtesy of Creighton Karas's crews. Now business is booming, and even with triple the space, we still have a waiting list.

Banner tried to pay for the rebuild, but I wouldn't let her. That's when she decided to make the loan to Nicole for Pints and Pins instead. Nicole, for the record, was not trying to buy drugs to sell to make meth. She had a cold and an expired license the night Banner and I saw her at the pharmacy.

Ben came forward as Memphis's anonymous tipster. He said he'd seen too many things happen in this town over the years, and he was sick of waiting for Timmons to get off his ass and figure it out. Now, he's officially retired and living in Florida.

Other people might have been changed by inheriting $30 million, but all Banner asked for was a woman cave to be built behind our house to hold her office. It ended up becoming a full-blown warehouse on the property to hold all the inventory she keeps in Gold Haven. She's since hired two full-time employees for shipping and administrative stuff, and Blush is already making a profit. She also started the Myrna Frances Memorial Scholarship at five different community colleges to help women who want to take business classes, one scholarship for each year Mrs. Frances was in her life.

To say I'm proud of her would be an understatement. To celebrate the one-year anniversary of her company, I surprised her with a fully restored cherry-red SS convertible with blush-pink pinstripes.

"Rose, do not put that in your mouth."

I turn to see Creighton Karas talking to his daughter behind me, which never ceases to amuse me. The man can run an empire, but his baby girl has him wrapped around her finger.

Holly has just started to show with their second. I can only hope to be so lucky.

"You about wrapped up, Bruce?"

All the women turn at my question as they prepare to start another vibrator race across the bar.

"Logan! Are you early?" Banner looks toward the clock on the wall.

"I'm an hour late, actually."

She smiles and waddles toward me. If she knew I even thought the word *waddle*, she'd crucify me. Even though I'd explain it's the most beautiful fucking waddle in the world.

"They're placing bets. Holly put fifty on a girl. Greer put fifty on it being a boy."

"Fifty dollars?"

Banner laughs. "Fifty thousand."

"Jesus Christ," I whisper.

"Don't worry, the loser has to contribute it to her college fund."

"Still a her?"

Banner rolls her eyes. "Of course. There's no way I'm wrong about this."

"I guess we'll find out soon, won't we?"

I grab her hand and lift it to my mouth to press a kiss against it. She wouldn't let me replace the ring from the arcade with a diamond, so I had a white gold replica made and swapped it out. Her finger is too swollen to wear it at the moment, so it's in the safe at home.

Banner smiles. "We might be finding out sooner than we thought. I think I've been having contractions for the last two hours."

"And you didn't call me?" My voice is calm, even though my head feels like it might explode.

"I was having fun."

"Bruce . . ." There are a million things I could say right now, but instead, I lift her into my arms and head for the door.

"We'll see you all at the hospital later," I yell.

"Don't forget to take your shower favors!" Banner calls over my shoulder. "They're my newest bullet vibrators and cock rings. I can personally attest to them being amazing."

Only my wife.

The best decision I ever made was to take that Road Runner to New York City myself.

Seventeen hours later

"Mr. Brantley, would you like to hold your daughter?"

I meet Banner's tear-filled eyes over the head of the tiny infant lying on her chest.

"Absolutely. Come here, Rogue."

The End

Click on www.meghanmarch.com/#!newsletter/c1uhp to sign up for my newsletter, and never miss another announcement about upcoming projects, new releases, sales, exclusive excerpts, and giveaways.

I'd love to hear what you thought about Banner and Logan's story. If you have a few moments to leave a review on the retailer's site where you purchased the book, I'd be incredibly grateful. Send me a link at meghanmarchbooks@gmail.com, and I'll thank you with a personal note.

Intrigued by Creighton Karas and Holly Wix? The Dirty Billionaire Trilogy is available now! Keep reading for a sneak peek of *Dirty Billionaire*.

CHAPTER ONE

Holly

*Country Star JC Hughes Caught Between a Cock and a
Hard Place*
*How is he going to explain this one away to girlfriend Holly
Wix and his fans?*

"That two-timin' son of a . . ."

I hiss under my breath as I stare at the headline—and the compromising picture accompanying it—splashed in vivid color across the front page of the gossip rag displayed prominently in the checkout line at my supermarket. For the second time in two months, it's a picture of my "boy-friend" locked in an unmistakably passionate embrace with another woman, except this time she's wearing a giant black strap-on.

The edges of the paper crumple in my sweaty grip, and I fight the urge to tear it to shreds, along with every copy sitting on the rack in front of me.

He's going to destroy my career before it even has a chance to become a reality.

One year, they said. One year in this joke of a "relationship" and I'd earn my stripes, be all set in the world of country music. Judge me all you want for agreeing, but when your brand-new record label puts something like that in the contract that will jet you out of the backwoods town you're dying to escape, you don't ask questions. You sign on the dotted line.

But reality is a cold slap in the face, and some days it hits you when you're standing in line at the grocery store. What happens when they finally catch JC with a guy? His habit of swinging both ways, but preferring men to women, is about to become the worst-kept secret in Nashville.

I'm Holly Wix, winner of a make-me-a-star TV show, and handpicked by the label to buoy JC's once-impressive but now flagging career. It didn't seem like a big deal when they slipped it into my contract in the beginning. What starry-eyed girl wouldn't be thrilled to have her name linked to a country star?

Instead of the one-way ticket to stardom I naively expected, I'm becoming the butt of every industry joke faster than the guys back home can spend their paycheck on twelve-packs and scratch-offs. But I've got one shot at keeping this dream career alive, and honestly, there's nothing I wouldn't do to save it. So this situation with JC needs to get settled before things spiral further out of control.

Tugging the bill of my trucker hat lower, I glance around to see if anyone has noticed me flipping out in the checkout line. A woman behind me clucks her tongue as she pulls her sunglasses out of her baby's mouth.

Crap.

That cluck of her tongue was aimed at me, not the toothless, blue-eyed, smiling baby. Surprisingly, though, the expression on her face is sympathetic, not angry.

"Men are assholes, am I right? Being famous just makes them bigger ones."

I smile weakly, and she continues. "Don't believe everything you read in the papers, doll. They're always ninety-five percent bullshit. Probably Photoshopped. He should have his head examined if he's cheating on you."

Snapping my gaze back to her, I read recognition all over her face, despite my hat, glasses, complete lack of makeup, and relatively low level of fame. I force a smile onto my face, but it feels awkward and fake.

"It's called a gossip rag for a reason, I guess?" I reply, failing at my attempt to inject some humor into my tone.

She nods and gestures to the half dozen bottles of wine in her cart. "This probably sounds crazy forward, but you look like you could use a drink and someone to vent to."

Vent to a perfect stranger I met in the grocery store? That would be insane, not to mention dangerous. If I did, the "she said" side of the story would be splashed all over tomorrow's papers, and the label would kill me—the painful death of breach of contract and being blackballed in the industry.

I already used up strike one the first time a picture of JC hit the papers. I marched right into Homegrown Records' offices and told them their devil's deal wasn't worth it, and that I wouldn't help JC's career at the expense of my own.

Their response? If I didn't turn around, march my ass

right back out of the office, and paste a smile on my face, they'd yank me off my tour, and I'd be a has-been before I ever got the chance to become a someone.

I'd go to bat for my career any day of the week, but faced with the threat of losing it, I'm ashamed to say I backed down and toed the company line. You only get one shot at your dream. It's not something I'm willing to let go . . . regardless of how much of my pride I might have to swallow. Which brings me back to the gossip rag and the woman in front of me.

An awkward silence stretches between us in the checkout line as all the scenarios swirl through my brain of how I can reply to her. Finally, she smiles, and there's something kind and knowing in her expression.

"I know what you're thinking—you can't spill your side of the story to anyone. Too risky." She lifts her hand and flashes a giant rock on her left ring finger. "But I'm not just anyone. I've been on the front page of the tabloids too, and I know exactly how much it sucks. After being married for a decade to the biggest reformed horndog of them all, I'm no stranger to any of it. On top of that, I'd never break the vows of sisterhood."

My gaze darts from the giant diamond to her face. Studying her makeup-free features, it finally hits me. "You're Tana Vines."

Tana Vines was the Female Country Artist of the Year about ten years back, and her husband was awarded Entertainer of the Year at least four or five times during that time. They're country music legends. A true power couple.

She holds out her hand and I shake it, operating purely on instinct.

"Yes, I am," she says. "It's nice to meet you, Holly Wix."

Two bottles of wine later, Tana and I lay sprawled on chaise lounges beside her indoor pool. Behind the gated walls, and in the presence of someone I listened to on the radio in junior high, I finally have a chance to unburden all the crap that has been filling my head for months.

"Six more months? That's a hell of a long time to put up with JC's bullshit. Not to mention keeping your own legs closed. Good Lord, girl. Aren't you dying to get some dick?" Tana asked.

An embarrassed laugh escapes my lips. "Um, I've been pretty preoccupied with learning the ropes, I guess."

"Well, shit. I'd be dying for dick."

I shake my head. "I don't want to do anything to jeopardize my position with the label. I have a feeling that if my picture ended up in the paper the way JC's has, the double standards would have me out on my butt so fast, I couldn't even yell 'Bingo!' first."

Tana rolls onto her side and faces me. "That's probably the truth, but it don't make it fair. The only reason they're covering his ass is the shelf of awards he's got from five years ago, and all the money they've got invested in him. You're the perfect image booster. But you're right—you're expendable if you step out of line."

I already looked up to Tana as a country idol, but now I have to say I have a bit of a girl crush. She doesn't sugarcoat anything, and it's refreshing in this world of people who say one thing and mean something completely different.

"Who's expendable?"

A deep voice echoes through the pool room as Mick Vines walks in. The man—a living country legend—picks up one of the empty bottles on the table between our lounge chairs. "And damn, Tana. I've been lookin' for you for a half hour."

"Gemma knew where I was." Gemma, I learned, was Tana and Mick's live-in nanny.

Tana sits up as Mick sets the bottle down and leans over to press a kiss to her lips.

"There. Been lookin' for that. My little bit a sugar."

I turn my head away as Tana wraps her hand around the back of his neck and pulls him in for another kiss, this one not nearly so innocent. She doesn't seem to care that I'm intruding on their intimate moment. And it's a moment that makes me wish even more that I wasn't trapped in this mess.

Not that I'm looking for what they have—because I'm truly not. I'm not looking for that kind of happily-ever-after for a good five or ten years. I'm too young for that, and my focus is on my career, exactly where it's supposed to be when you're standing on the edge of achieving the dream you've had since you were ten years old.

But even on that edge, I'm still only a puppet with the label pulling the strings. Six months in, and I'm already sick and tired of being yanked in the directions they want me to go. What could I accomplish if only I could cut those tethers and come into my own? But slicing those ties would mean sacrificing what I've already accomplished, and that's not an option.

Mick stands tall again and notices me for the first time.

"Who's our guest, babe?"

It's much less of a surprise that he doesn't recognize me than it was for Tana to make the connection. Honestly, I'm still a nobody in this industry. I'm working my tail off on becoming a somebody, and I've got fans, but to someone at Mick Vines's level, I'll always be a nobody.

I smile and hold out my hand. "Holly Wix."

His eyes narrow as he shakes my outstretched hand. "I've heard your name. Why have I heard your name?"

I'm stunned that there's even a hint of recognition in him. My stomach turns in big flopping waves, and Tana jumps in, saving me from bumbling whatever explanation is about to fall from my lips.

"I picked up Holly in the checkout line while we bonded over how much it blows to see yourself on the front of a gossip rag."

Mick's gaze narrows further before it lights with knowledge. "Wix. You're the hot young thing JC Hughes has on his arm these days."

I cringe at the description, because that's not how I want to be known. *But that's what happens when you sign a deal with the devil.*

Tana slaps his thigh from her seated position. "And she's touring with Boone Thrasher because she's the hottest new talent to hit the stage since Carrie and Miranda."

Her adamant statement throws me for a loop, and those nervous waves in my belly glimmer with pride.

Mick rocks back on the heels of his tooled black leather boots. "Ain't heard her sing yet, but I've sure seen her picture."

I wince, pride doused.

"And that's the problem. The label has backed her into a corner, and they've made the JC situation a requirement. She can't get out of it," Tana explains.

Mick studies me. "Who you with, girl?"

"Homegrown. They signed me when I won *Country Dreams*."

"Ah." Mick nods twice. "Now I know where I first heard your name. And you probably signed a devil's bargain to get your 'million-dollar recording contract' after you won."

It isn't even a question. Mick knows how the game is played.

"It was that or keep working at a bowling alley in BFE, Kentucky, and never taking my shot. At least this got me to Nashville."

He raises a hand. "No need to get defensive. I'm not judging. We all take the route we need to take to get here, but that means living with the consequences. How long are you stuck with this JC bullshit? I'm assuming you have to suck it up and smile on his arm to help shine up his image and get some good press. Besides, we all know he's been on the edge of casino-playing retirement for a more than a few years now."

Dang. Mick really does know how the game is played. I guess you couldn't be in Nashville as long as he has without learning all the pitfalls.

"Six months," Tana offers. "And it's not like when our managers hooked us up. JC doesn't seem to care either way if he hurts Holly's career."

I swivel my head around to stare at Tana. "I didn't know that you . . ." I glance back to Mick. "Really? Your relationship started out as a publicity stunt?"

Tana laughs. "Of course it did. Why else do you think I'd get involved with such a man-whore? I needed some street cred, and he was getting all the wrong kinds of press for sleeping with everything with tits."

"Jesus, baby. That's ancient history—and we kept that shit quiet for a reason."

"I'm just saying that sometimes it actually works out fine," Tana says.

Mick shakes his head. "Back to the point of this conversation." Aiming his stare at me, he continues. "You could be fucked in six months if JC keeps this shit up. You've got sympathy on your side right now, but if you keep laying down and taking it, you're just going to look like a fool."

Tana slaps his thigh again. "Not helping."

Her husband reaches down and grabs her hand. "Quit, woman, or I'll spank your ass even harder tonight."

Tana's face flushes a bright red, and I decide to let the comment go without trying to figure out exactly what they're talking about.

Mick releases her hand and grabs the magazine shoved between the wine bottles. "This the rag with the cheating dick?"

Shaking her head, Tana grabs it from his hand. "Nope, that's the one with the hot billionaire dick I'm going to marry if you decide to leave me for some country starlet."

I catch a glimpse of the cover. It's a copy of *Forbes*, and there's a stupidly handsome dark-haired man on the cover.

The headline reads: CREIGHTON KARAS CRUSHES COMPETITION.

"What are you talking about, woman? You'd bury me out back if I so much as looked at another woman," Mick grumbles.

Tana's lyrical laugh echoes off the walls. "Damn right, and don't you forget it."

I snatch the magazine out of his hand to get a closer look.

"Whoa, girl. Calm down."

I wave him off, the wine dulling the instincts that would otherwise have me continuing to bow and scrape in his country-music royalty presence.

"Shhh. I need to look at him." I'm not sure why I need silence to do that, but apparently the large bottle of wine I drank says I do.

The man is gorgeous, but he looks cocky and arrogant. I flip the magazine open and page through it until I find another picture of him.

I win because losing isn't an option.
—Creighton Karas

I know I'm truly drunk when the only thought filtering through my brain is how much I'd like to be his prize when he's winning. *Where the hell did that come from?* And like I'd even know what to do with a man like that. He's so far out of my league, it's not even funny.

I glance over at Mick and Tana, who are once again locked in a tangle of lips and limbs.

And . . . that's my cue to leave.

I slap the magazine shut and rise on shaky legs. "I should probably get going."

Tana pulls away from Mick and raises an eyebrow in my direction. "Honey, you ain't driving anywhere. I'll go make up a guest room. It's the very least I can do since I got you shitfaced."

"Not necessary. I should get home. I have . . . a plant that needs water. Or something."

I squint because I can't remember if my plant is dead or alive. I haven't watered it in as long as I can remember. Apparently I'm thinking too hard about plants, which might be alive or dead, and not concentrating on my balance because I tip forward.

Mick catches me with an outstretched palm. "Come on, honey. We're putting you up tonight. Won't hear anything different."

He turns me around and marches me toward the door that leads into the sprawling mansion. "Besides, it seems like someone needs to take you under their wing so you don't get chewed up and spit out by this bitch of an industry. My wife isn't exactly the type to bring home strays, so she must've seen something in you needing a little protection. We're gonna make sure you have it."

My eyes burn, and I blink back the unexpected tears. I've been in this town for six months, essentially friendless, and in one night I've apparently been adopted by two people I never thought I would ever have a chance to meet.

"G'night, Holly. I'll see you in the morning, sweets," Tana calls from behind me.

Apart from those blissful moments standing onstage, for the first time in months I have a genuine smile on my face, and I feel like I belong somewhere.

It doesn't last long.

Also by Meghan March

Beneath Series:
Beneath This Mask
Beneath This Ink
Beneath These Chains
Beneath These Scars
Beneath These Lies
Beneath These Shadows

Flash Bang Series:
Flash Bang
Hard Charger

Dirty Billionaire Trilogy:
Dirty Billionaire
Dirty Pleasures
Dirty Together

Dirty Girl Duet:
Dirty Girl
Dirty Love

Bad Judgment

ACKNOWLEDGMENTS

I've never laughed so hard while writing a book. Logan and Banner's story poured out of me, and I hung on for the ride.

Thank you to the amazing team who helped take my words and turn them into a final product of which I'm incredibly proud.

Angela Marshall Smith, the first reader of my words. Your insight is invaluable, and I'm blessed to have you in my life.

Pam Berehulke, editor extraordinaire. Thank you for being so incredibly fabulous in everything you do.

Angela Smith, for taking this crazy ride with me and helping me to keep it all running smoothly. Have I told you lately that I love you?

Danielle Sanchez, publicity goddess. Thank you for handling your job like the boss you are.

Natasha, Jamie, and Stacy, rock-star beta readers. Thank you so much for your feedback and your time. I appreciate it so much more than you know.

Hang Le, amazing cover designer, for once again flexing your creative muscles and delivering exactly what I need.

My Runaway Readers Facebook Group, I feel privileged to have such an amazing crew of ladies and gents who show such passion for my books on a daily basis. Love you all.

My readers, you deserve all the thanks and gratitude I can offer. Without you, I wouldn't have the most amazing job I can possibly imagine. How about we keep doing this thing, yeah?

Fabulous bloggers, for reading and promoting all of these words solely for the love of books. You are the backbone of this indie book world, and don't receive nearly enough credit for all that you do. You are appreciated. You are effing fabulous.

JDW, the epitome of a *real good man*. I could fill an entire book with all the reasons I love you, and am so fucking lucky to have you in my life. I can't wait to see what adventures we're going to have next.

And as always, *my family*, for cheering me on every step of the way.

All my best,
Meghan

AUTHOR'S NOTE

I'd love to hear from you. Connect with me at:

Website: www.meghanmarch.com
Facebook: www.facebook.com/MeghanMarchAuthor
Twitter: www.twitter.com/meghan_march
Instagram: www.instagram.com/meghanmarch

UNAPOLOGETICALLY SEXY ROMANCE

ABOUT THE AUTHOR

Meghan March has been known to wear camo face paint and tromp around in the woods wearing mud-covered boots, all while sporting a perfect manicure. She's also impulsive, easily entertained, and absolutely unapologetic about the fact that she loves to read and write smut.

Her past lives include slinging auto parts, selling lingerie, making custom jewelry, and practicing corporate law. Writing books about dirty-talking alpha males and the strong, sassy women who bring them to their knees is by far the most fabulous job she's ever had.

She loves hearing from her readers at meghanmarchbooks@gmail.com.

Made in the USA
San Bernardino, CA
30 January 2017